TALE OF
TWO DOLPHINS

TALE
OF TWO
DOLPHINS

HORACE DOBBS

JONATHAN CAPE
THIRTY-TWO BEDFORD SQUARE LONDON

First published 1987
Reprinted 1987, 1988
First published in paperback 1988
Copyright © 1987 by Horace Dobbs
Jonathan Cape Ltd
32 Bedford Square, London WC1B 3EL

A CIP catalogue record for this book
is available from the British Library

ISBN 0 224 02409 4 (hardback)
0 224 02618 6 (paperback)

Printed in Great Britain by
Butler & Tanner Ltd, Frome and London

CONTENTS

	Foreword	11
1	The Hunt for Percy	15
2	Donald in France?	27
3	Dolphin Link	43
4	Percy Reappears	52
5	Assignment Adventure	66
6	A Closer Encounter	82
7	A Robinson Crusoe Day	95
8	Disaster Strikes	105
9	Dolphin Intelligence	119
10	The Magic of Dolphins	134
11	Paradise Bay	143
12	Percy Exposes Himself	155
13	Percy Becomes Assertive	162
14	Percy Rules	169
15	A Gift from the Gods	181
	Postscript	188

ILLUSTRATIONS

between pages 32 and 33

1-2 Percy at Portreath.
  3 Jean Louis in Brittany.

between pages 64 and 65

  4 Pakistani fisherman painted on the
    Pelletiers' vehicle.
  5 Stained-glass window designed by Lynne
    Emmerson depicting Jean Louis.
  6 Jean Louis over the kelp forest.
  7 Percy lifting an anchor.

between pages 96 and 97

  8 Percy and the author off Godrevy Island.
  9 Percy as seen by Judy Holborn.
 10 Percy and the 'Dobbsophone'.
 11 Percy and the *Tar dor Moor*.
12-13 Percy and Jean Louis playing with anchors
    and anchor chains.

between pages 128 and 129

14-15 Percy playing with the catamaran.
 16 The Dolphin Link group enjoying their
    Polynesian life-style.
 17 Carola Hepp and the mural she designed
    and painted.

between pages 144 and 145

 18 Upside-down canoist meets Jean Louis off
    Brittany.
 19 Percy looks at the author's fins.
 20 Percy and Laurie Emberson at play.
 21 Percy above water.
22-3 Percy and Tricia Kirkman establish contact.

This book is dedicated to all those who have been
touched by the mysterious magic of dolphins.

He who binds to himself a Joy
Doth the wingéd life destroy;
But he who kisses the Joy as it flies
Lives in Eternity's sunrise.

William Blake

Foreword

Dolphins and humans have a special relationship, one potentially stronger than that between humans and any other animal. Just what it is that places dolphins in their unique position in our affections has intrigued me for over a decade, and I first started to unravel it when I met Donald, a friendly wild dolphin, off the Isle of Man in 1974.

One of the characteristics that immediately endeared Donald to me was his irrepressible sense of fun. Many animals, particularly young ones, have this general quality – a family of kittens playing together, a group of lambs frolicking in a field. But Donald had an attribute they didn't. Donald had a sense of humour, and a sense of humour is something very personal, varying from one individual to another. It almost certainly originates in the higher centres of the brain, and it implies an understanding of a particular human's psyche. We derive no pleasure from telling a joke to someone who possesses no sense of humour. Until I met Donald, I regarded a sense of humour as a trait exclusive to humans.

This discovery stimulated me to an even greater interest in what went on in a dolphin's mind. I wanted to find out what Donald was thinking, and to do this I devised a number of experiments, all depending on Donald's voluntary cooperation. By circumstances that seemed to defy all statistical chance I was able to locate the dolphin and swim with him. I have to admit, however, that once I got into the sea with Donald I found it extremely hard to keep to any preconceived plan, because of his complete disregard for the seriousness of my work and his apparently avowed intention to reduce everything I did to a jolly jape. There were many times when I thought our roles were reversed, and that Donald was studying me as much as I was studying him.

Donald's studies of me started the first time we met, off the Isle of Man, and continued throughout an odyssey which included stops in Wales and ended in Cornwall. During his sojourn in the West Country I was fortunate enough to make a television film with Donald. After completing it I devised an experiment which, if successful, would demonstrate that dolphins and humans could work together voluntarily to perform a task under the sea. However, that experiment was never put to the test. After making contact with some friends of mine on my birthday, 14 January 1978, Donald vanished.

I was distraught. The more I reflected on what I had done with Donald, and on the effect he had had on me, the more I wanted to pick up where we had left off. I had shown part of the Yorkshire Television film about Donald at a presentation in Buckingham Palace, and Prince Charles had expressed a desire to swim with the dolphin. Ever hopeful that Donald and I would meet again, I maintained a constant look-out for reports of human–dolphin encounters which might indicate that he had moved to a new location.

When I heard about a friendly wild dolphin in the Red Sea I knew it couldn't be Donald, but I was flattered when one of the first divers to swim with the dolphin named him Dobbie after me. I went to see my namesake, and after a long search under a scorching sun located him off Coral Island, near Eilat.

I estimated the underwater visibility to be about 150 feet. From the sea bed, 40 feet down, I watched the dolphin rocket to the surface, leap high into the air, plunge back into the sea again and then glide down to within a few feet of me. We got some dazzling footage of him silhouetted against the sun, which sent shafts like searchlights beaming into the sea. It could not have been a greater contrast to my meetings with Donald in the cold waters off the British coast. In the Red Sea bikini-clad girls, who snorkelled down to see the dolphin, pirouetted in the water and returned to the surface to gasp for breath. They dived down again and again. It was like a beautiful ballet.

As soon as I met the Red Sea dolphin I felt as if I had known him for years. The relationship we immediately established was completely different from that I had had with Donald two years previously. Whereas my brief friendship with Dobbie was extremely gentle, Donald had excited me. Dobbie had an aura of gentleness and serenity. Although he swam very fast when he jumped, by the time he was back with me on the sea bed his movements were slow – indeed he seemed to flow through the water with almost no movement of his tail at all.

My encounter with Dobbie was beautiful but brief. Shortly after my return home I had a letter from Israel reporting that the dolphin's body had been washed ashore – riddled with bullets.

The more I searched for friendly wild dolphins, the more incredible in hindsight my experiences with Donald became. Indeed, I sometimes speculated that without film evidence of our relationship many people would have thought I had dreamed up the episode.

After the last sighting of Donald in 1978 I continued to appeal for information on friendly wild dolphin connections. By 1980 my grapevine of contacts was so extensive that I felt I could safely assume that news of friendly approaches by solitary dolphins would eventually reach me from anywhere in the world. Which indeed they did. Snippets of dolphin information found their way to me, often by the most tortuous and unexpected routes, but most referred to brief encounters, further contact being lost after a few days or a few weeks. An analysis of all known long-term contacts between humans and wild dolphins produced a microscopic figure in comparison with the total population of dolphins. For much of the time there was nothing – anywhere in the world. As the data piled up I resigned myself to the prospect that the likelihood of meeting another friendly wild dolphin like Donald was almost infinitesimal. Perhaps in ten years if I was lucky, or twenty, or perhaps never. I couldn't say.

Then, late in June 1982, I had a message that changed everything. A friendly wild dolphin had been spotted, and not on the other side of the world but in Cornwall.

The first thought that came into my mind was 'Donald's back!'

· I ·

The Hunt for Percy

The news was broken to me over the phone by a professional diver with a rich Cornish accent. Keith Pope had been on holiday for a week, and on Sunday, 6 June, 1982, took the opportunity to make a last fun dive before going back to the more serious business of salvage work. With the help of his longstanding diving buddy, Colin Pike, and a neighbour, Paul Noble, whose job was to look after the boat while the others were diving, Keith launched his inflatable into the harbour at Portreath. It was high tide. The sun was shining and the sea was flat calm. The plan was to dive at Gull Rock, about half a mile from the harbour entrance, where the two divers hoped to pick up some lobsters for an end-of-holiday supper.

Here is how Keith described what happened:

> With the harbour behind us, I had my outboard full throttle and was soon planing at 20 knots, when suddenly Colin shouted and pointed to a black fin coming towards us at incredible speed. The fin then disappeared under the boat. No sooner had it disappeared than a dolphin surfaced right on the bow, like a figurehead; it seemed as if it was part of the boat. 'It's Beaky!' I shouted.* 'He's back!' We had both dived

---

* Beaky was the name sometimes given to Donald, the wild dolphin whose antics off the Isle of Man first came to my attention in 1974. The full story of Donald alias Beaky is told in my book *Follow a Wild Dolphin* and its sequel *Save the Dolphins*.

many times with Beaky, the friendly dolphin, and now after six years he had returned.

I immediately throttled back and stopped, but he was gone. Then, suddenly, the dolphin shot out of the water about four feet into the air, seeming to hang there for a split second before crashing under-water again. Colin and I tanked up and were soon standing on the sea bed ten metres down, both waiting for our old friend to come into view. He soon came, circling us seven or eight times at a distance of about fifteen metres. We both then realised that it was not Beaky at all. Beaky was at least two feet longer, and this dolphin didn't have Beaky's characteristic scars.

I picked up a spider crab and held it out, hoping our friend would come in close to inspect it, but he was still a little apprehensive and never came closer than about five metres. He had, it seemed, a continuous grin on his face, with an expression that said 'Come and get me if you can.'

Colin and I carried on with our dive, staying down around thirty minutes with the dolphin coming in several times. On our return to Portreath we finally saw our friend following a small fishing boat, the skipper on VHF loudly informing all surrounding craft, 'You won't believe this but I've got a dolphin on the bows.'

I felt I had to try to meet the new friendly dolphin, even if it turned out not to be Donald, and so on Tuesday 13 July, my car laden with cameras and diving equipment, I set off from Yorkshire to Cornwall. It was a hot, sticky day, and the air was humid with heavy fog when I stopped in the dark on Bodmin Moor to telephone Keith. He had volunteered to meet me on the main road at the turn-off for Portreath as the route to his house was complex.

When we arrived I was introduced to his attractive wife and children before being taken on to my bed-and-breakfast, which had the romantic address of Beach House, Smugglers' Cove, Portreath.

Beach House lived up to its name, and it was run by long-term friends of Keith, Judy and Bob Holborn, who made me feel very welcome. I was given a room overlooking the sea, and when I opened the window as wide as it would go I could see the silhouette of Gull Rock rising mysteriously off the inky blue-black water. I wondered where the dolphin was and what he was doing. Would I be able to find him? Lulled by the gentle rhythm of the sea as it surged on the beach below, I soon fell into a deep sleep.

When I awoke the next morning, the table in front of the window was covered with droplets from the rain that had poured down during the night. The sea was blue-grey, slightly rough, and Gull Rock had a necklace of white foam round its base. I scanned the water with my binoculars, watching the boats entering and leaving the harbour at Portreath, since I knew dolphins enjoy playing around moving craft. But there was no sign of a playful dolphin. Previous experience had taught me how fruitless it can be just to go out to sea in a boat in the hope of finding a wild dolphin, so I decided to do some reconnaissance, driving along the coast and looking out from headlands, but expecting to get the most productive information by chatting to anyone and everyone who might have seen him.

At first most people were vague about their sightings. However, when I persisted with my questioning many of them were able to relate their observations to other events, and thereby come up with more precise times and dates. I felt like a detective, trying to track down the movements not of a wanted man but of a much wanted dolphin. By the end of the day I had a good idea of the dolphin's territory around Portreath. Even though I had not seen anything myself, I felt I had made a good start.

The following day the sea was rough and the sky grey. The surf pounding on to the beach at Portreath was fine for the surf riders but very bad for me, because spotting a dolphin surfacing briefly in a rough sea is extremely difficult, and keeping track of his subsequent movements virtually impossible. I spent the day doing more detective work. In the evening the weather cleared and I enjoyed sitting on the cliffs looking for the dolphin and watching the light sparkle on a ruffled sea which became progressively redder as the sun sank towards the horizon. That night, after a barbecue supper, Bob and Judy had a gathering at Beach House of some of their friends who had seen the dolphin. I showed one of the films I had made for television, *The Magic of Dolphins*, to the assembled company, and afterwards we had a stimulating debate during which I described a few of my adventures with Donald. I was delighted to learn that my host, Bob, had also swum with Donald and was keenly interested in the new friendly dolphin.

In order to avoid confusion I suggested the new dolphin should be given a name. 'How about Percy?' I proposed. 'Portreath Percy sounds good,' came the response from one member of the audience. 'Right,' I said. 'Then henceforth Percy he shall be.'

As soon as we had given him a name, Percy took on a character, and by the end of the evening I had built up a very strong image of him. I was able also to establish some of his movements during the week before my arrival. It seemed, for instance, that at about 7 p.m. on 7 July the dolphin had come into the bay at Portreath. There were no boats around. He had made some spectacular leaps, apparently for the sheer joy of it, and much to the pleasure of those watching from Beach House, before heading north and out of sight. On the following day, at about 8 p.m., he streaked past a fishing boat entering Portreath and then vanished. On Friday, 9 July, he was seen – through binoculars, far out at sea near Godrevy Island – about six miles from Portreath.

There were no reports for Saturday, but on Sunday evening Percy was back in Portreath playing just outside the harbour entrance with a fishing boat. The skipper, Alan Vine, whom I came to know well, was pulling in pots aboard his quaint orange-hulled boat, the *Tar dor Moor*. Inside one of the pots was a small conger eel, which Alan tossed over the side. Quite by accident it landed on the head of the dolphin, who was taking a keen interest in these strange human activities. This caused Percy to slap his tail vigorously on the water, drenching Alan and his crewman Jack Gristwood, who told me the story. The two fishermen found the incident highly amusing, and they said they felt certain the dolphin enjoyed the joke too.

Although I had seen Donald swim in and out of a trawl, I knew some fishermen did not like dolphins, because they thought they would damage their nets, and partly because they were a source of competition for fish. I was delighted to learn that a local fisherman was not only tolerant of the dolphin, but even enjoyed having his company when out potting for crabs and lobsters. Indeed, Percy seemed to be taking quite an interest in fishing boats, for on the following evening at 8.30 he was again seen in Portreath, this time following a fishing boat 100 yards off the harbour entrance.

There were no reports of the dolphin being seen the next day. Knowing the purpose of my visit, and having a keen interest in the dolphin himself, Bob Holborn had spent much of the following day out searching for Percy – but without success. That was Tuesday 13 July, the day of my arrival in Portreath. Thus by the Thursday evening of my film-show three days had elapsed without a sighting. Was this another of those brief encounters in which dolphins make contact and vanish without trace? I hoped I hadn't just missed Percy, as I had missed the dolphin called Sandy in the Bahamas. Keith Pope, who had first contacted me, volunteered to take time off work the following day and take me out to sea to look for the dolphin. As his boat had a powerful engine, he said we could cover all the places where Percy had been sighted. The prospects looked good, for by the time I went to bed the sea had calmed down. I could hear through the open window of my bedroom the waves gently murmuring on the sandy beach. It was a wonderful night. And it heralded a perfect day.

I woke to hear Bob calling excitedly. He had seen the dolphin in the bay, making a single, spectacular leap. The sea was absolutely flat and we both scanned its surface with binoculars. But there were no more leaps and no tell-tale appearances of a fin as the dolphin surfaced to take a breath of air. 'Sorry, Horace. He's gone,' apologised Bob. 'But he *was* here, I promise you.'

For the next hour I kept glancing out to sea, but Percy did not reappear. After breakfast I met Keith Pope at the harbour in Portreath. Dressed in our wetsuits, we loaded our diving gear into his inflatable boat and cruised slowly to the narrow harbour entrance. Once there, we had to decide which way to go – west towards Godrevy Island or east towards St Agnes Head. We decided on the latter course. The powerful engine brought the boat up on to the plane, and soon we were skimming across the water at a fine speed. Keith loved driving his boat, and I enjoyed the spectacular beauty of the Cornish coastline with its towering cliffs. A light wind rippled the surface of the sea, the tiny waves scattering the intense sunlight into countless flashes that hurt our eyes as we looked intently for any sign of the dolphin.

I knew, however, that our greatest chance of making contact depended not on our finding Percy, but on Percy taking an interest in us and coming to ride in our bow wave.

We looked at the changes in the colour of the water as we moved eastwards along the coast, and Keith told me what the areas were like to dive. At midday we landed on a tiny secluded beach with no access from the land. It was one of Keith's favourite picnicking places. Keith was very tough. He wore a single gold earring and, like many Cornishmen, had to live on his wits and his initiative. Earning a living wasn't easy, and I doubt he would have missed many of the bonuses that providence passed his way. He was a modern-day buccaneer, but at the same time he was sensitive to the beauty and vulnerability of the creatures that inhabited the sea. For a while we clambered together over the rocks, following one of my favourite pastimes – beachcombing – before continuing our search for Percy.

Off a point called Sally's Bottom we came across a small fishing boat. Keith quickly zoomed alongside.

'Have you seen the dolphin this morning?' he asked.

'Yes, about half an hour ago. He came around the boat and then headed west.' The fisherman was pointing back towards Portreath.

'Thanks,' said Keith, as we headed westwards at high speed.

'Do you think we passed him without noticing on the way to St Agnes?' I asked.

'We could have done – we were going fast,' he replied.

Near the harbour at Portreath we encountered another small fishing boat. Gliding alongside, we spoke to the fisherman who was hauling in a string of pots.

'Have you seen the dolphin?'

'Yes,' came the reply. 'He was with me ten minutes ago.'

We were getting closer.

We cruised gently westwards towards Gull Rock. Just as we were rounding the island, which was crowded with sea birds, there was a swirl alongside. Percy had found us. He popped his head briefly out of the water, as if to say 'Hello', and then vanished beneath the sea without a ripple. A few moments later he surfaced on the other side of the boat.

I had my fins, mask and snorkel at the ready. Putting them on, I slipped over the side of the inflatable. The visibility under-water was about fifteen feet. Immediately, a grey shape with its tail pumping up and down passed like a torpedo at full speed across my field of view and vanished into the haze. I was in murky water, and the dolphin, a sinister battleship grey in colour, was travelling at great speed. He was much larger than I, and capable of dealing me a death blow by ramming me with his powerful beak. Yet I felt no menace. During that fleeting moment, as he passed by, I had registered an image of the dolphin's face, with its jaw-line set in a permanent, gentle smile. But it was the look in his eye that reassured me. I felt an overwhelming sense of excitement as I hung motionless in the water, peering intently into the haze, waiting for Percy to reappear. There was no point in attempting to swim after him, because he could outpace me and vanish with two flicks of his tail. The next pass was slower and closer. Then he came towards me, head-on, and stopped about five feet away. Looking up at me, Percy said in a body language which I immediately understood, 'How about a game?'

I finned quickly towards him. In an instant he turned, and, with a couple of pumps of his tail, vanished into the haze once again.

I knew I couldn't catch him, but I was infected with his playful spirit and set off in hot pursuit. It was to no avail, of course. A few seconds later he came up and passed at speed from behind, clearly demonstrating his superiority in every sense. It was a game in which we were as unmatched as a cat and a mouse. I could only hope I would not suffer an undignified demise, with my corpse being tossed in the air, the usual outcome of such one-sided games. To prove I wasn't a run-of-the-mill swimmer, I duck-dived and swam down towards the forest of dark green kelp that covered the rocks beneath me. This immediately appealed to Percy, who obviously enjoyed having another dimension added to the area of play. He circled me at speed and disappeared. I stayed down for as long as I could. When I returned to the surface, gasping for breath, he came up alongside, flicked his tail in the air and submerged again, as much as to say, 'Come on – let's go down again.' I stayed in the water, joyously swimming with Percy while Keith cruised gently around in his boat. The dolphin did not confine his attention exclusively to me, however, and made frequent trips to Keith in the inflatable. When another inflatable came out from the beach Percy had a further diversion.

Then Keith and I changed places. It gave me a great sense of pleasure to see a fully grown man, a professional diver who had to spend many hours working in the water, jump into the sea and play in a totally uninhibited, childlike manner with the dolphin. Watching the two of them frolicking together reminded me that one of the characteristics that sets dolphins apart from all other animals –

including man – is that they enjoy physical play even into old age. A sense of simple non-competitive fun and games is a characteristic few humans retain as they pass from childhood to the cynical years of middle age. I felt it was one of the many lessons the dolphin had to teach us when we ultimately acknowledged that we could possibly learn something from the other large-brained inhabitants of our planet.

The occupants of Beach House had been watching our antics from the shore, and it wasn't long before Bob Holborn launched his own inflatable and was ferrying his guests out to see the dolphin. The more boats and activity there were around him, the more Percy seemed to enjoy himself. Although he paid us several visits as we swam and cruised slowly around Gull Rock we could not retain his attention for more than a few moments before he sped away to cavort with the increasing number of people swimming on the surface and eager for his attention.

We stayed in the bay and played with Percy whenever he chose to come to us. Eventually Keith anchored his boat and we put on our diving equipment in order to stay under-water with the dolphin. I have made hundreds of dives in British waters. As I descended I once again enjoyed the sense of freedom that comes with drifting like a feather down into the sea and breathing with a regular rhythm. The underwater visibility of about fifteen feet added another dimension to the pleasure. It was the sense of mystery that went with not knowing what lay just out of sight beyond the ever-present mist of sand and plankton that hung over the underwater landscape. Out of that green, sun-illuminated haze the grey, graceful shape of the dolphin would appear and vanish. Because of the optical effects of the water Percy's size was magnified by a third. Allowing for this illusion, I estimated his length to be between nine and twelve feet. This would mean that Percy was a mature dolphin.

By the time we had finished our dive Percy had gone, so

we cruised back into the harbour at Portreath which was just a short distance away.

That evening I met Keith again at a splendid dinner prepared by Colin's wife Ollie. We reviewed the situation and concluded that the dolphin preferred to play on the surface. Keith was still obviously very pleased he had found Percy and that we had been able to spend so much time with him. Red-faced from the sun, the excitement and the wine, I went to bed a very happy man.

Before setting off for Portreath I had made contact with my filming partner, Chris Goosen, with whom I had sought, found and filmed a dolphin in the Red Sea. Chris came down to the West Country, but although he had been helping me with my reconnaissance during the previous three days he did not come out with me in Keith's boat on Friday. When Saturday dawned, crisp and clear, he was keen to get out to sea to meet Percy, and to film me under-water with the dolphin. Percy, however, had other ideas. Despite the brilliant sun and flat-calm sea, we saw no sign of him. Keith took us to all the places where the dolphin had been seen previously, but to no avail. Percy had once again moved elsewhere.

Even so, we spent an enjoyable day at sea. Our excursion included a run through a narrow opening in the sheer cliff wall close to Portreath at a location the locals called Ralph's Cupboard. Once through the gap the sea opens up into a roughly circular pool at the base of an immensely high cliff that rises like a gigantic chimney. When we entered, many of the seabirds nesting on the ledges high above rose in the air, squawking loudly as they took flight. The sound, magnified by echoes from the surrounding cliff walls, swelled and then slowly died as the birds became accustomed to our presence far below. The sea was turquoise blue and every detail of the sea bed beneath the inflatable could clearly be seen.

That evening we learned that while we had been searching for Percy near Godrevy Island and in other places west of Portreath, the dolphin had moved east and spent the day entertaining the holiday-makers in Perranporth – which was eight miles to the north-east.

However, to make Chris's visit to Cornwall worth while, the dolphin came back to Portreath the following day, Sunday, and my partner got first-hand proof on film of the elusive friendly wild dolphin. Filming Percy above-water was difficult because we never knew where he would surface. As he darted from one source of interest to the next it was particularly frustrating to hear the cry, 'Look, there's Percy! What a fantastic jump!' – for by the time Chris had swung his camera round to where the action was the dolphin had completed his leap and was back under the sea. We both knew from experience that, despite the technical difficulties of filming under-water, it was easier to get longer sequences when diving with Percy. Even so, when we got into the water we obtained no more than a few feet of useful film because visibility was not very good and the dolphin never stayed within range for more than a few seconds.

It was not until 9.30 that night that I set off to drive the 450-mile journey back to my home in Yorkshire. I did not feel at all tired. I was very excited and my adrenalin was running at a high level. Between cassette tapes of music, which I played at high volume, I reviewed the situation. I would never forget the look of jubilation on Keith Pope's face when we first spotted Percy after failing to make contact for three days. When I succeeded in taking some still pictures as the dolphin surfaced alongside a fishing boat, he had put his arm round my shoulder and said, in his delightful West Country brogue, 'I told you I'd show you a wild dolphin didn't I? Well, there he is.' His phone call to a complete stranger who had travelled half the length of Britain on the chance that he might see a wild dolphin was vindicated. I told him how immensely grateful I was that he should have taken the trouble to contact me. I was absolutely delighted that the outcome of my visit should have been so successful, and I told him just a few of my hopes for the future.

As a direct result of Keith's call I had succeeded in

making contact once again with a friendly wild dolphin who was obviously interested in human company, and who was especially playful with those who were prepared to get into the water. However, Percy would not approach too close and certainly would not permit physical contact. So we had a long, long way to go before we could get to the stage I had reached with Donald, who after three years had allowed me to handle him in almost any way I wished. But my plan was to go beyond that, and attempt not just to stimulate interest in play, but to gain the dolphin's active cooperation. To do that I had to gain a far greater understanding of what went on in the hidden and unprobed depths of a dolphin's mind. Only then could I hope that we might put into practice my long-term ambition, which was to join forces with these intelligent creatures in exploring and understanding the sea. However, it has often been said that a long journey begins with the first step. As I drew into the drive of my house at first light the following morning I knew that I had made a good start. But where would that journey lead me, and the others who had been touched by Percy's magic?

Although we were unaware of it at the time, the arrival of the dolphin was to have a profound effect on the lives of two people who were completely different to one another in almost every respect. One was Bob Holborn, a powerful swimmer and the possessor of a first-hand knowledge of the sea gleaned from many diving experiences. Bob was an extrovert who was always joking, and his boyish pranks made life for the guests at Beach House lively and amusing. Public relations, he called it. The other was one of the guests at the house. The mother of three children, she was as slender as a bamboo pole, and her dark eyes had the bright, nervous look of a hunted deer. She would sit alone, her arms crooked around her knees, and stare wistfully out to sea between curtains of waist-length black hair. Too shy to ask Bob to take her out in the boat to see Percy, she dreamed of the wonders beneath the waves that she would never see because she couldn't swim and was terrified of the sea. Her name was Tricia Kirkman.

Donald in France?

On Boxing Day, 1982, a young man sat down and wrote me a letter. In it he described how he and some friends, while surfing at a place called La Baie des Trépassés in Brittany during the summer of 1981, had been joined by a dolphin who played with them in the waves. The author of the letter, Andy Crofts, had been to the same bay several times but had seen the dolphin only once. He assumed that the dolphin had just been passing through, although he did think it unusual as he knew that dolphins normally congregate in groups called schools, or pods. The following year he returned to France to spend two weeks canoeing with a group of friends in the same area. During the second week they saw a dolphin playing with the lifeguard's boat. They were delighted when on the last two days of their holiday the dolphin joined them as they paddled their canoes out to a nearby headland. His letter continued:

> We spent some time both days playing with him in canoes and with snorkelling gear on. He was about ten feet long and looked quite old and battered with many scratches and marks on his body. One distinguishing mark was a nick in his dorsal fin. I enclose a picture of him. Anyway we had to return as most of our group had work commitments, but I decided to find out about dolphins. On reading your books, which I have recently discovered, I became intrigued by the case of Donald and I began to wonder if he was the same dolphin I had met.

> The picture enclosed, which was taken under-water, had

a blue cast. It showed the left-hand side of the dolphin's head. Donald had been shot at close quarters and the resultant wound had left a depression, but on the right-hand side of his head. Thus I couldn't say whether the dolphin in Andy's picture was Donald, although the description in the letter fitted him very well. Had the old rascal left Cornwall and joined the Common Market I wondered? I was desperately keen to find out more about the friendly wild dolphin off the Brittany coast, but when I telephoned Andy his mother informed me that he was away skiing and wouldn't be back until the end of January. However, she did tell me that the dolphin was extremely friendly, that all the members of the canoe group from Imperial College had got in the water with him, and that he had been very playful. The French dolphin certainly did sound very much like Donald.

Following up the correspondence from Andy Crofts, I received from Caroline Tombs, a fellow student of Andy's, a more detailed account of the 1981 encounter, as well as a description of a further encounter in July 1982. She had accompanied six members of the Imperial College Canoe Club to Brittany. Here is her description of the second encounter:

We camped for a week at La Baie des Trépassés, a sandy beach enclosed by a rocky coastline with deep, clear water. The bay, usually battered by thundering surf, was quiet and peaceful due to a persistent anti-cyclone in the Atlantic. Conditions were idyllic; we abandoned surfing and took to sunbathing, snorkelling, windsurfing and paddling around the coastline.

Every day the lifeguards zoomed across the bay in their inflatable, and after a day or two we noticed a lone dolphin leaping in its wake. This in itself was very exciting to four of us, who had never seen a dolphin in the wild; meanwhile, the other three were busy wondering if their old surfing companion had come to visit them.

On 22 July, with two days left to go, Andy and I pulled on our wetsuits and got in our canoes – short surf boats with white, flat bottoms. As usual, the sea was flat as we paddled out of the bay towards a small, rocky harbour where a few yachts were moored and we had seen divers.

As we approached the harbour, I felt rather than saw a sleek, grey fin lift out of the water, no more than two metres from my boat, and heard a great 'whoosh' of expired air; just as suddenly, the great body vanished. My reactions of fear and incredulity were quickly dispelled by a jubilant Andy, who immediately began to paddle furiously in the direction which the dolphin had taken. 'He's playing with us!' he yelled – and indeed he was, in an elaborate game of hide-and-seek which lasted an hour. The dolphin would swim slowly, surfacing far more frequently (we later found out) than necessary, allowing us to approach within a few feet, then dive and shoot at high speed in another direction. Sometimes we were baffled by his disappearance, until we realised, with a surge of exhilaration, that he was underneath us, just a few inches below our boats – we think now that he was fascinated by the white canoe hulls, thinking maybe that they were the bellies of some strange aquatic creatures.

Towards the end of the first session we discovered a new game: we would capsise, hanging upside-down in the water, and the dolphin would swim up towards us, nearly touch noses, then swoop away. Eventually, exhausted, we decided to leave and paddled back to the shore. The dolphin followed us close in-shore, then turned out to sea again.

As we beached, the others, puzzled by our strange antics, were preparing to set out and investigate. When we reported our experience, they immediately set off to find the dolphin. Andy and I quickly forgot our exhaustion, flung canoes, masks, snorkels and flippers into the van and drove to the harbour to meet them. The dolphin was in the harbour with the five canoeists, playing the same hide-and-seek game, rushing madly from boat to boat. Andy and I put on our snorkelling gear and slipped into the water for the greatest game of all. As we started finning and diving, the dolphin approached and dived with us, often within touching distance. Sometimes we were diving in complete synchronisation, surfacing and diving together, as the dolphin deliberately slowed his pace to ours.

During this time we were able to have a closer look at our companion, and Andy became convinced that he was the same dolphin that they had met in 1981. He was the same size, around ten feet long, had several scars, and the same distinctive nick in the dorsal fin. In this second encounter, which lasted about two hours, all seven of us exchanged snorkelling gear to dive with the dolphin. We tried the capsising game, wearing masks, and were able to clearly see the dolphin approach from below as if to touch the glass with his beak – fantastic! Again, sheer exhaustion drove us away.

Two days later we had to leave, after one more play session with 'our' dolphin. Surfing wise, it had been a disastrous trip, but we agreed that we had all had one of the most wonderful experiences of our lives. We are positive that the dolphin deliberately approached and consciously played with us in an attempt to communicate. We were aware of some emotional involvement which we could not put into words – only a vague feeling of upheaval, and great tenderness.

There was nothing in Caroline's sparkling description of her holiday to indicate that the dolphin in France was not Donald – whereas his behaviour was absolutely typical of the dolphin whose departure I had mourned since 1978. So was the French dolphin Donald, or wasn't he? There was one certain way to find out – go and see for myself.

Although I enjoyed a great deal of freedom I felt I couldn't just pop to Brittany on the very remote chance – especially after a winter of stormy seas – of meeting the dolphin. So when my wife Wendy suggested we take a spring holiday in Brittany, combining sight-seeing with dolphin-hunting, my conscience was eased.

On 1 May, 1983, having enjoyed the early morning celebrations in Oxford and listened to the bells of Magdalen College, we continued our journey south. In Oxford we had been joined by one of Wendy's friends, Cathie, so it was with two female companions that I drove to Portsmouth where we were to catch the ferry to St Malo.

By mid-afternoon the following day, in bright sunshine, I was driving down the small winding road that led to La Baie des Trépassés. I turned a bend, and there revealed before me was a long, lovely strand of yellow sand upon which ranks of glistening waves hurled themselves. I could understand why Andy and Caroline had come here to ride the foaming white surf. It was just off this beach that first contact was made in 1981. From a sketch map Andy had kindly provided me with I identified a rock standing out to sea. That was where in 1982 links were made. Close to the beach, with a good vantage point from which to view the rock, was a modest hotel – Hôtel de la Ville d'Ys, the hotel of the town of Ys (the sea queen). Although the hotel stood safely high on a sandy bank, legend had it that in ancient times the town of Ys from which the hotel was named was below the high-tide line, and that marine lock gates kept the sea out, or let it in. Ys was governed by Gadlon, King of Cornwall. The town flourished and became rich. But with opulence came debauchery. The king's beautiful but cruel daughter was persuaded by a prince to give him the silver keys of the sluice gates. When the jealous prince saw the princess with other lovers he opened the sluice gates at high water. The princess was consumed by the sea and became Morganez – the Breton mermaid.

With such colourful associations, I was delighted to be told that the Hôtel de la Ville d'Ys had rooms available which were well within our modest budget. Furthermore, the one Wendy and I were allocated looked straight out towards the rock. As soon as I had put the cases down I pushed open the windows and the shutters. Immediately, the door behind me crashed shut with a tremendous bang as the wind coming straight off the sea rushed through the room and into the corridor. I shut the windows and looked out to sea through my binoculars but could see no sign of the dolphin among the waves around the rock. Near to the small island, however, was a headland from which I knew I could get a much better view.

Leaving my wife to unpack, I scrambled to the top of the rocky promontory as fast as I could. The strong on-shore wind channelled upwards by the cliffs buffeted me so hard I couldn't keep the binoculars steady, so I lay on the ground and scanned the sea swirling round the rock. Then, to my amazement and utter delight, a dark dorsal fin appeared just for a second in my field of vision. Surely my eyes were deceiving me. I couldn't be so lucky as to spot the dolphin within a few moments of my arrival. But I was. Seconds later my sighting was confirmed – I saw the grey mass of a dolphin's back arch out of the water and return to the sea in a single, smooth, graceful sweep. I lay on the ground and thumped the turf with my fist in uninhibited jubilation. 'I've seen him. He's here. I've found him ...' I could not have been more excited if somebody had told me I'd won a fortune on the football pools. I stayed watching the dolphin cruise gently round the rock before bounding down the path to break the news to Wendy and Cathie.

During the night I listened to the wind rattling the windows. At 6.30 a.m. I was looking out through my binoculars to see if I could spot a dorsal fin. The wind had dropped considerably and not a cloud was to be seen in the bright zircon sky.

But the beautiful start to the day was misleading. As we consumed our bowls of coffee, and loaded butter and confiture on to freshly baked bread, the clouds were gathering. By the time I had got myself kitted up with wetsuit and aqualung the sky had completely clouded over. By the time I launched myself into the sea from a rocky ledge over which waves irregularly poured, it was 10 a.m.

1 My first contact with Percy off Portreath – exciting but fleeting.
2 Percy became progressively more friendly, and the following
    year he posed for this picture.

3 At the interface of two worlds – a meeting with Jean Louis.
(*photo: Georgie Douwma*)

To conserve my air supply, I inflated my life jacket and swam towards the rock, breathing through my snorkel tube and peering from side to side. I could see threads of plankton suspended in the grey-green water. Beneath me was a dark, eerie world, the deep green fronds of the kelp plants absorbing the light. I had seen underwater scenery like it many times off the British coast.

Dolphins can hear extremely well under-water. I called out 'Donald, Donald' through my snorkel tube – just as I always did in the past when I wanted my dolphin friend to come and say hello to me. But no cheeky face appeared out of the misty water. I took my knife out of the scabbard on my leg and, holding it by the blade, banged the handle against the bottom of my air cylinder. The sharp clunk it made carried a long way under-water, and was one of the identity sounds I used to attract Donald. Still the dolphin did not appear.

With an estimated body weight of about 700 pounds and a need to consume about 5 per cent of that weight a day in fish, the dolphin needed to catch and eat about 35 pounds of fish every day. As was usual in the area in which I was swimming, there were very few fish about. It would be far easier for the dolphin to feed off the nearby headland where shoals of fish would congregate to feed on the food carried along in the strong currents. As I journeyed towards the island I hoped that the reason for his non-appearance was that he was away feeding.

When I reached the island I put the mouthpiece from my regulator into my mouth, deflated my lifejacket and allowed myself to sink slowly down into the kelp forest. A few wrasse fish meandered between the stems of the kelp fronds that grew like the trunks of miniature palm trees from the rocky sea bed. I swam along a gulley and the forest closed over my head. There were trails of coarse sand between the boulders on which sea urchins, which are so aptly called sea hedgehogs, browsed. An edible crab was tucked into a cranny in the rocks, and a couple of spider crabs crawled on long articulated legs between the kelp stems with the slow, deliberate movements of robots. Drifting, weightless, in a chasm dividing this forest of branchless trees, I could have been a spaceman looking for a friendly alien on another planet – which in some ways I was.

After about an hour in the water I started to feel cold. I shivered, as much from disappointment as discomfort. During my stay in the water I had been making sounds and willing the dolphin to appear.

Deciding to abandon the hunt, I surfaced close to the island, intending to conserve what air I had left in my cylinder. I snorkelled back towards my entry point, but when I was about half-way there I came upon an aluminium float marking a wooden crate used for storing crabs and lobsters. The bottom half of the float was festooned with small, bright green seaweeds. I decided to make one last attempt to attract the dolphin, and once again took the diving knife from its scabbard and hammered the aluminium buoy with the knife handle.

The sounds cracked through the water like pistol shots. I put the knife back in its holster, and was just about to swim the final leg to shore when a grey, smiling face appeared in front of me. After keeping me waiting for an hour Donald had responded to my call.

But was it Donald?

No, it wasn't.

One look at the face peering curiously at me answered the question that had puzzled me ever since I had received the letter from Andy Crofts. The dolphin that came up to me was about the same size as Donald. Like Donald, he was covered with marks and scars, but he did not have the depressions on the head which marked Donald's major wounds. Also, I was able to discern a distinct personality difference. Whenever I had re-made contact with Donald after a period of absence, his arrival had had all the vigour, excitement and unpredictability of a cavalry charge. The French dolphin was much more restrained – a more gentlemanly dolphin, I felt – but then, that was perhaps because we were unacquainted.

The grey skies that threatened rain had deterred all other visitors to the tiny bay. I was entirely alone with the dolphin and felt completely uninhibited. I talked to him. Told him how pleased I was he had come to say hello. He responded by swimming round me and then vanishing, only to reappear a few seconds later with a quick pass that openly expressed in body language the message 'You can't catch me.' I responded by diving down and doing somersaults in the water, and my new-found companion looked on with an ever-present hint of amusement on his face.

But whereas my friend was coated in a super-efficient warmth-retaining layer of blubber, I was protected by only six millimetres of foam rubber. After cavorting with the dolphin for half an hour I was forced by the cold to leave the water. The dolphin followed me right to the rock, where I slowly clambered out, the weight of my air cylinder and weightbelt adding to the problem of remaining balanced while wearing fins and being pushed and pulled by the swell that surged over the sharp rocks. It was an extremely undignified exit, made even more cumbersome by the fact that I was beginning to get hypothermic, which impaired my strength. I was also very tired. But my high spirits gave me the strength to climb the cliffs to my car, where I thankfully dumped my aqualung and 18-pound weightbelt in the boot of the Citroën before driving the short distance back to the Hôtel de la Ville d'Ys. Too weary to bother with changing, I plodded through the hotel in my dripping red wetsuit. Being French, the guests taking coffee at the tables I had to pass between took no notice. In my bathroom I peeled off my wetsuit like a banana skin and plunged into a tub of steaming, scented, foaming water. With images of the wild dolphin still swimming around in my mind I lay in the bath revelling in the sheer, unadulterated pleasure of feeling the warm water in contact with my naked body. After a long immersion in a cold grey sea a hot bath is a sensual experience beyond compare – especially when supplemented with a noggin of Cognac.

During a protracted and gastronomically excellent lunch

I chatted in my schoolboy French with the lady who ran the hotel. Occasionally we were interrupted by one of her menagerie of animals demanding attention. These included a Siamese cat with a stub tail and a very large dog with tiny ears, one of which was permanently bent down. They had free range over the entire hotel, including the dining room, the cat often picking her way delicately between the place settings on the tables. It was a very French hotel.

I told Mme Barbeoc'h about Donald. When I produced some photographs of him she became very animated and passed them to the drinkers who crowded round the bar. She informed me that my new friend had been in the same area for several years, and that his name was Jean Louis. Her daughter often swam with the dolphin. I later discovered that my hostess had led a life as colourful as that of the legendary Breton mermaid, Morganez. According to one of the locals she was sent to hospital with a terminal illness but willed herself to get better when she learned that her husband was philandering in her absence. On the way back to the hotel to convalesce after her illness she seduced her attendant in the back of the ambulance and openly proclaimed him as her lover to teach her husband a lesson. Her husband, a man with a magnetic personality who attracted many famous people to the hotel, died shortly afterwards, and Annette Barbeoc'h continued to run the establishment with the aid of her family. Even before I learned that Annette had conducted her earlier years with such Gallic bravura I was aware of her strength of character and enjoyed the openness with which she expressed her feelings – especially those towards Jean Louis.

After lunch I drove to the Cap du Raz, just a few kilometres away. It was then that I realised the immense similarity in landscape between Brittany and Cornwall. The Cap du Raz is the most westerly part of France, a French Land's End. It has a huge car-park, souvenir shops and a network of well worn paths that vein the rocky granite promontory. Just as at Land's End, coaches pour in and disgorge their loads to swarm like ants along the nearby trails. The visitors have their photographs taken with the wickedly treacherous sea and rocks and the lighthouse in the background. Little did they know that just a short distance away a friendly wild dolphin was playing among little fishing boats.

On the way back to the hotel I turned the car radio to the weather forecast from the meteorological office and heard that gale force eight winds were blowing up towards Cape Finisterre. Undeterred, I changed into my wetsuit in the hotel and drove again to the little bay beside Dolphin Rock, as I had now dubbed the tiny island where I first met Jean Louis. It was 6.30 p.m. by the time I got back to the water's edge. Fortunately the ever strengthening wind was blowing off-shore, which meant that despite the white horses that now covered the sea, it was relatively calm closer in.

The landscape was empty. It was pouring with rain. Was Jean Louis waiting for me? I slid quietly into the water and submerged. The sea was considerably clearer than before and I found myself swimming through a mass of sand eels, wriggling like tinsel streamers. I was pleased to see them. They would provide food for the fish that Jean Louis would feed upon. They would also provide him with an hors d'oeuvre. I finned slowly forward, the bubbles from my life-support system gurgling comfortingly to the surface. Looking up, I could see the pockmarks made by thousands of raindrops falling on the silver roof over my head. They made no sound. It was strangely peaceful under the sea compared with the squally, wind-tormented environment above. I felt warm, safe and comfortable. I loved wandering through the green seascape on my own, not having a diving buddy to worry about, accountable to no one and hoping that I would meet a fellow solitary traveller from another planet.

Within a few minutes of entering the water, my wish was granted. A silver spaceship cruised gently into view. From a distance Jean Louis' scars were not apparent. The dark grey of the superstructure melted into the white underside of a sleek animated machine that flowed through the water without effort. He escorted me through gulleys in the underwater forest, watching me curiously as we went, matching his mood to mine.

Jean Louis was much larger than I was, and I knew that locked away in the barely moving tail was enough power to send him rocketing out of the water – or to project him head-first into the side of a large shark with such force it would be killed instantly. So much power was awesome to contemplate, yet I felt in no way threatened or afraid because it was controlled by a friendly alien who was not destructive, did not kill his own kind and dispatched sharks only if they threatened his family. As I swam alongside I thought how marvellous it would be if he would share some of his secrets with me and we could explore the oceans together. I tried to communicate my thoughts to him as he took me on a guided tour through the seaweed jungle that covered the rocky undersea crags around Dolphin Rock. Jean Louis did not allow me to approach too close, somehow managing to maintain the separation between us without moving away. It was as if he could position himself wherever he wanted to be without effort, whereas I had to resort to finning frantically with my legs if I wanted to move at even a modest speed. Not that I really tried to make contact. I was content to fin quietly and enjoy the company of my undersea guide with the gently smiling face.

The time I could spend under-water was limited by the supply of air in my cylinder, which had been half full when I started. By swimming gently I stretched it to over half an hour and programmed my undersea tour so that I was back at my entry/exit point when my air supply finally ran out. Jean Louis stayed with me until the end. I thanked him as I prepared to climb out, and told him I would return.

Brittany is justly famous for its crêperies, which serve delicious pancakes with a great variety of fillings, both savoury and sweet. 'La Brochette' in Plogoff was our haven that evening. It was an old cottage, with flagstone floor and beamed ceiling, that had been converted into a restaurant. We arrived dripping wet as the hostess Louise Praugnaud was about to shut for the night. Despite the fact that we were the only guests, she piled logs on to the open fire and served us a superb meal to the accompaniment of the wailing wind and rattling windows. Outside, the gale was raging at full strength and rain was lashing the stone walls. After the meal she and her husband, who was the cook, joined us for drinks and we sampled the local liqueur made from wild strawberries.

The storm spent itself during the night and the next morning I climbed the rocky headland overlooking Dolphin Rock. It abounded with spring flowers freshened by the rain. Right on the top, nestling between the rocks, were clumps of dwarf bluebells, which up until that time I had always thought of as being woodland flowers. Yet here they were, mixed with the cushions of pink thrift on a headland exposed to fierce sea winds. From the headland I caught occasional glimpses of Jean Louis cruising round Dolphin Rock far below. Within a short time I was back snorkelling in the water with him. I had found and part-filled a tin with pebbles. This was to be the underwater rattle with which I could announce my arrival to Jean Louis and which, hopefully, he would identify as my special sound signal. It certainly worked. Within a few minutes of my slipping into the sea the dolphin was alongside, gazing intently at my simple underwater sound generator. I snorkelled out towards Dolphin Rock with Jean Louis darting around for company, quite excited with my rattle. Then, in deep water, I accidentally dropped it. At the same time Jean Louis disappeared. I had lost both my rattle and the dolphin. I swam around tapping everything in sight with the handle of my knife but Jean Louis did not return. On the assumption that he had gone fishing I went back to the hotel and took my wife and her companion on a tour of the countryside.

When we returned in the late afternoon I immediately changed into my wetsuit and returned to the sea with a new tin of stones. But despite swimming right round Dolphin Rock, rattling my tin as I went, I saw no sign at all of Jean

Louis. I gave up the search after half an hour and climbed to the top of the headland to see if I could spot my friend. Through my binoculars I scanned the bay beneath me and the sea around Dolphin Rock; then I switched my gaze to the distant headland of the Cap du Raz with its old-fashioned lighthouse and reef extending far out from the headland. A fleet of fishing boats were working the waters between the rocks that stuck out of the sea like irregular, black teeth. Even if I never saw Jean Louis again, I realised how lucky I had been to have made contact with a dolphin in such a vast expanse of shimmering water. When I considered the hundreds of miles of coastland of Brittany and Cornwall, the fact that I had found and swum with two friendly wild dolphins within one year seemed even more remarkable.

The following day, Thursday, 5 May, was the last of our brief visit to Brittany. I got up very early and climbed the headland. Once again there was a keen, cool wind blowing which buffeted me as I reached the summit. I had my binoculars but didn't need them. I could see Jean Louis gently swimming around Dolphin Rock in a grey sea. I thought I would be the only person around at that early hour. But on the rocks close to the water's edge I could see two anglers were already fishing. I scrambled and ran between the rocks and down the path back to my car, hoping that Jean Louis would not go off fishing before I could get in the water and say goodbye. In a couple of minutes I had undressed and donned my wetsuit. I belted my heavy weightbelt around my waist, slung a couple of cameras around my neck, and bounded towards the steep slipway clutching my fins, mask, snorkel and a tin of stones.

I swam on the surface vigorously towards Dolphin Rock rattling the tin. Before I was a hundred yards off-shore Jean Louis was alongside. I threw my tin of stones away: I didn't need a code signal, Jean Louis would recognise me anyway. The dolphin came up and stayed directly in front of me with his beak just a foot from my facemask. I could see both his eyes looking intently into mine. I stretched my arms forward in Y formation and he came even closer. We both stayed quite still. I wished I knew what he was trying to communicate.

Suddenly, his eyes flash. He moves away. The spell is broken. I snorkel down and he starts to get excited, following me into the eerie green depths. I swim up and the dolphin comes up with me. Just as I reach the surface he accelerates and launches himself high out of the water. For a split second I am aware of a silver arch and a dripping cascade over my head. Then he plunges back to the sea a few feet away from me. Consumed with excitement I dive down again, turn, and then swim upwards finning as fast as I can with every ounce of energy I can muster. I burst through the surface and manage to get half of my body out of the water. At the same moment Jean Louis flies through the air over my head and crashes into the sea beside me again. The rest of the world doesn't exist. The dolphin and I are alone in a bubble of explosive energy. I turn in circles, do somersaults under-water, swim on my back, swim on my front with the dolphin stroke, splash the water with my hands and lash the surface of the sea with my rubber fins. Jean Louis reacts vigorously, swimming in tight circles around me in a riotous game without rules.

The game finished when I ran out of energy and had to lie on the surface of the sea, gasping for breath through my snorkel tube. Jean Louis became calm and moved slowly away. When I had recovered I went in search of my playmate and found him swimming gently up and down an anchor rope, letting it rub over his abdomen. As he did so, I was able for the first time to see his entire underside clearly. Were my eyes deceiving me? Could I just detect two mammary slits? I swam very slowly down so as not to get the dolphin too excited. I succeeded. He continued to rub himself against the anchor rope, and just for a moment I was able to register the details on the white belly. I could see the anus, and a very short distance from that the slit concealing the urinogenital opening. Close to that orifice were two more well-concealed small openings, one on either side.

I knew that behind those slits were hidden the mammary glands. Beyond a shadow of doubt Jean Louis was female. How on earth had I not become aware of it before?

I later discovered how the dolphin got her name. Apparently, Jean Louis is a name commonly used for sharks by Breton fishermen. When a local fisherman saw a fin cutting a path through the water towards his boat he cried out, 'Jean Louis! Jean Louis!' Of course, it wasn't long before he discovered his mistake, much to the amusement of his fellow fishermen. None the less, the name stuck – even when it was discovered that the dolphin was female. As I always found it difficult to remember when to use *le* and *la* I was quite pleased to have an example to quote which clearly demonstrated that the French were not really bothered by discrepancies in sex or gender.

When I had recovered from my surprise I wondered if I should re-name the dolphin Jeanne Louise. But I decided against it on the grounds that it would be presumptuous of me to change a name that those who knew the dolphin far better were happy with.

I stayed in the water with Jean Louis for an hour and ten minutes, taking photographs and playing with her, sometimes vigorously, at other times very gently. I regretted leaving her after such a brief but memorable encounter, and as I left Brittany a few lines from a poem by Philip Larkin flitted briefly into my thoughts:

There is regret. Always, there is regret.
But it is better that our lives unloose,
As two tall ships, wind-mastered, wet with light,
Break from an estuary with their courses set,
And waving part, and waving drop from sight.

Would Jean Louis and I meet again, like wandering ships?
Fate already had that matter well in hand.

· 3 ·

Dolphin Link

A few days after getting the letter from Andy Crofts I was
given a ticket for the London Boat Show. I went there to
discuss leading a diving expedition to the Red Sea with a
friend who was looking for a new yacht. After we had
completed our business amid the gleaming, multi-
thousand-pound luxury boats I managed to navigate
through jostling crowds to a cubby-hole of a stand with a
display of photos of Polynesian-style catamarans for the
do-it-yourself sailor whose pocket was smaller than his
dreams or his enthusiasm. There I met James Wharram. He
was already known to me as a maverick who led a very
unconventional life-style and eschewed the entrenched
Western concepts of sexual morality and monogamy. His
way of life was greatly influenced by extensive studies and
knowledge of Polynesian culture. James's alternative life-
style included wearing the minimum of clothing – or,
whenever possible, nothing at all. Not surprisingly, this
often raised the hackles of the uniformed gold-braid
brigade who regarded James as unsavoury and decadent,
but whose life-style, I suspect, some of them secretly envied.
However, James preferred not to engender unnecessary
hostility. At the Boat Show he appeared in the one respect-
able suit he kept for such occasions.

Our exchanges were terse but significant. He thought his
catamarans could be used to provide cheap floating bases
for scientific studies of the oceans. A mutual friend, Wade
Doak, was already using a Wharram catamaran in New
Zealand for a dolphin study called Project Interlock.

'Horace,' he said finally. 'I am over fifty. I can design catamarans with my hands tied behind my back. I have one big project left in me. It has to be with dolphins. Will you help?'

Although I didn't go along with all James's philosophies, I did find refreshing the freedom of thought and expression they embodied, so I agreed. We jointly devised the Dolphin Link Project, which was revised several times until we defined our objective as the designing and building of a catamaran that could be dismantled and freighted anywhere in the world. It would provide a relatively cheap base, and would be sailed by what James termed 'sea people' who were close to nature. We hoped the dolphins would identify and associate with a vessel and people that harmonised with the sea, and thereby give those on board a chance to observe the hitherto secret and private lives of a dolphin family. It was important that those on board did not try to impose themselves on the dolphins, who would be free to move away any time they wished to break the 'interlock' (the word coined by Wade Doak for interspecies communications). The boat would be sailed in regions frequented by dolphins, but it would be up to the dolphins to come to the boat. In other words, the dolphin could initiate the encounter (for such a meeting Wade invented the word 'dint' – or dolphin initiated interlock).

When the ideas for Dolphin Link were being assembled I envisaged the first contact with dolphins being made in a gentle manner in warm tropical seas. But circumstances conspired against this dream. After formulating our ideas for the Dolphin Link Project James Wharram made his first link with a wild dolphin in one of the most dangerous and treacherous stretches of water in the world. This came about as a result of my encounters with Jean Louis in La Baie des Trépassés.

In order to progress with my own studies, which would lead to a cooperative relationship between humans and dolphins, I wanted to attempt some experiments with a friendly wild dolphin in the open sea. To do this required that I should first establish a close, friendly relationship with a dolphin and then progress as fast as circumstances would allow towards my set objectives. To finance such a study was completely beyond my resources, but in the past I had overcome this difficulty by combining my objective with making a commercial film. This provides a film record, in unpredictable circumstances, of what happens, and can prove of great benefit when analysing the results. It also puts at the disposal of the researcher the technical resources of a film crew. These include the services of the film director's personal assistant, who is invariably extremely efficient at organising food, accommodation, bottle charging and the hire of boats etc. Technical experts, such as the sound engineer who can usually be persuaded to volunteer to help rig up the experiments as well as do his job of recording sound, are also on hand. Making a film also means making a commitment.

As soon as I returned from my visit to Jean Louis in France I knew that she could provide the central figure for a fascinating television film. At the same time I could do my experiments. Within a few days of getting back to England I had drafted a scenario and sent it to John Gau, who I knew was looking for ideas for a new television series he was putting together for Channel 4.

John Gau liked my proposal, and when he visited my house in the company of Peter Gillbe, who would be given the task of directing the film should it go ahead, we debated the chances of its success. On the negative side was the indisputable fact that I couldn't guarantee the film crew would even see a friendly wild dolphin, let alone get sufficient footage to make a compelling fifty-minute documentary. Set against that were the pictures I had taken of Jean Louis and my track record. Also, as a film maker, John Gau was in the risk business. I argued that making a film about finding a wild dolphin was only a little bit riskier than recording an expedition climbing a mountain. However, I had to concede the point that although the outcome of the climb was uncertain one could at least be sure that the mountain wouldn't just vanish.

I told John and Peter about James Wharram. Then I played my ace. I suggested I might combine my studies of Jean Louis with the Dolphin Link Project. There would not be time to complete the design of a new vessel, but if James Wharram were to sail one of his existing catamarans to La Baie des Trépassés it would provide a platform from which the objectives of the Dolphin Link Project could be put to the test. There was one small possible hindrance to my proposal. La Baie des Trépassés, or the Bay of Lost Souls, did not have such a dramatic name for nothing. The waters surrounding the Cap du Raz were among the most dangerous and treacherous in the world. Would James be prepared to take his boat and an inexperienced crew into such waters?

There was another factor to be taken into account. The only months in the year when it is really suitable for underwater filming in the North Sea are June, July, August and early September. And as everyone who has ever taken a summer seaside holiday in Brittany knows, even during these months good weather cannot be guaranteed. We were already in June. If we went ahead, could we assemble all the necessary people and equipment in France within a few weeks? Most important of these from a filming point of view was an underwater cameraman. With the proviso that all these logistical problems should be resolved, John Gau agreed to allocate the necessary funds and put a dolphin film in the list of subjects for his *Assignment Adventure* series.

I knew Peter Gillbe would have to exercise tight control over the budget, and since full film crews are horribly expensive to hire it was important for him to work out how, when and where he could deploy the camera team most effectively. It was arranged that we should make a quick reconnaissance trip to Brittany to assess the location. If after this visit Peter felt the film project was not viable, it would be cancelled.

I set off on Friday, 8 July, 1983 to drive to Gatwick, hoping that Jean Louis would live up to expectations. It was a roasting hot day with a clear blue sky, but as I parked my car at the airport a few drops of heavy rain smacked on to the roof. Peter and I flew to Quimper, collected a hire car and drove through the warm, neat French countryside to Plogoff, where we booked a table at 'La Brochette' before continuing on through the gathering dusk to La Baie des Trépassés. We were welcomed to the Hôtel de la Ville d'Ys by Annette Barbeoc'h, who gave me the same room as before, with a direct view from the window of Dolphin Rock.

We quickly deposited our bags and returned to the crêperie where Louise told us excitedly that the dolphin was in fine form. She had heard reports that on that very day several children had been in the water with the dolphin, and that she had put on a most spectacular display of leaps when a diver from England went into the sea. She said it was like a show in a dolphinarium. Such a glowing and unsolicited testimonial was more than I could have asked for to get the reconnaissance visit off to a good start.

When we returned to the hotel I stood by the window watching the flashes of the Cape Finisterre lighthouse. There was no wind. It was warm. The only sound was the irregular beat of gentle waves lapping the beach. As I looked out at the dark silhouette of Dolphin Rock, wondering what Jean Louis was doing, another image came to mind. It was a memory of Portreath, of standing by the open window at Beach House and looking out at Gull Rock.

There was a great similarity between the two locations. Was it just coincidence, I wondered, that the only two friendly wild dolphins in the world should have chosen two places with so much in common? The similarities were not just geographical, but extended to the landscape and the local people, many of whom consider they have more in common with the Cornish people than with their fellow countrymen in Paris. As an ethnic group, the Bretons did indeed have connections with the Cornish which dated back to Roman times, when the advancing armies stopped before over-running Brittany and the West Country, as well as Galicia in Spain, and Wales and Scotland. As a result, the Celtic tribal groups in these areas remained undivided, undiluted by their conquerors. Despite the rapid mixing of populations that has taken place in this century, regions like Cornwall and Brittany are still rich in Celtic families.

I once discussed this connection with a fellow dolphin devotee, John Tacon, who pointed out that a land and its people sometimes have an overall character that we can identify with, but often find hard to define. We say a place has 'a good feel'. In the so-called 'primitive' cultures, such as those of the Australian aborigines, the people live very close to the forces of nature, and define different parts of the terrain they roam as 'good' or 'evil'. It would not be unreasonable to suggest that certain highly evolved animals, such as the dolphin, do likewise. And at one time, during their evolutionary past, the dolphins were land animals. Perhaps they were able instinctively to make some kind of contact with the spirits that gave rise to the myths and legends abounding in Cornwall and Brittany since pre-Christian days. It was a romantic notion. But both Cornwall and Brittany are romantic places...

When I looked out of the same window the next morning the sea was illuminated with a soft yellow light that filtered through a thin veil of mist. In the circular field of my binoculars I could see Dolphin Rock, but beyond that the sea disappeared into the mist, which cleared only on the horizon. As a result, a yacht sailing far away appeared to float on air above the rock. It was a peaceful, magical cameo. I refocussed my binoculars on the water close to the base of Dolphin Rock, and at that very moment a familiar dorsal fin rose smoothly out of the water. I was going to thump on the wall to tell Peter next door to look at the sea, when the shutters of his bedroom opened and another pair of binoculars appeared. We leaned out and discussed the morning. I must admit to having a feeling of great satisfaction at the appearance of Jean Louis exactly on cue. However, as later events were to show, she wasn't prepared always to turn up just when I wanted.

She made the first of her non-appearances just after breakfast that same day. We took the car the short distance to the cove beside Dolphin Rock and watched a group of rubber-suited snorkellers diving down in search of crabs which they put into net bags. The water was very clear, and we could see Jean Louis following them round like a retriever dog. I got kitted up and, with a still camera around my neck, clambered over the rocks and slid into the sea just as the other divers left the water. Perfect timing, I thought. Now I should have Jean Louis' undivided attention. I spent half an hour snorkelling around Dolphin Rock, hammering everything in sight with my knife handle, but to no avail. If the dolphin had been nearby she would certainly have swum up to me. She must have gone off feeding.

I climbed up the rocks to rejoin Peter, but as soon as I had changed back into dry clothes Jean Louis reappeared and meandered aimlessly amongst the boats in the cove. 'You can't win them all,' I said, smiling at Peter. We sat chatting and watching as Jean Louis swam around a boat that was being moved on its moorings. Then the dolphin disappeared. A few moments later a boat came motoring towards the bay from about a mile away, escorted by a dolphin on the bows. I pointed out to Peter that I had observed this behaviour often with Donald. He seemed to adopt a territory with well-defined boundaries, and if any vessel intruded within those boundaries he went to investigate, escorting it until it stopped, or went out of his territory.

When the boat came in and dropped anchor, those on board jumped into the sea to play with the dolphin. Thinking I might get some nice pictures, I put on my wetsuit again and scrambled back into the sea. By the time I had snorkelled out to the group Jean Louis had disappeared. I called up to Peter on the cliffs, who scanned the sea through his binoculars and told me that Jean Louis was miles away, having a lot of fun playing with two windsurfers. I waited for half an hour and then gave up. Just after I had got dressed, I looked down on to the tiny sheltered bay. There, swimming among another group of snorkellers, was the friendly, fickle dolphin. Typical female, I thought.

Jean Louis disappeared during the afternoon, and we went on a brief reconnaissance trip. It was a perfect summer's day and the beach at La Baie de Trépassés, which had been completely deserted when we awoke, became filled with day trippers. We returned to the hotel and from my bedroom watched the sun starting to sink. There was no sign of the undersea inhabitant of Dolphin Rock. 'If only a boat would come into her territory,' I thought, 'Jean Louis would appear.'

Somebody on high must have been listening. At that moment an inflatable zoomed across the bay and did some turns in the middle of Jean Louis' territory. Those on board were obviously looking for the dolphin, and the Zodiac went to another outcrop of rocks, just as I would have done, and disappeared into a gulley. When the inflatable reappeared and sped into the bay Jean Louis came with it, performing several spectacular leaps on the bows. I waited until the rubber boat tied up to one of the mooring buoys, dressed once again in my wetsuit, and Peter ferried me to the cove in the hire car.

I spent over an hour in the water rattling and banging every conceivable object that would make an underwater sound. Finally, just as I was about to swim back to the shore, a cheeky face appeared alongside me. It was too dark to take underwater pictures, so I just swam around Dolphin Rock in the gently rippling sea, painted red and orange by the setting sun, with Jean Louis for company, like two friends out for an evening stroll.

We had arranged to see a local fisherman in the cove, so early the next morning I donned my wetsuit and was joined by Jean Louis as soon as I jumped into the sea. When the fisherman arrived and sculled out to his tiny fishing boat I escorted Jean Louis to this new source of interest. Peter

Gillbe was also in the boat, and I chatted to him as I floated in the water, wondering what to do next. Eventually I decided to go down into Jean Louis' undersea world. The mooring buoy and its rope were covered in green algae, and I pulled myself down the line, with Jean Louis following and watching intently everything I did. I pirouetted in the water and swam down further with Jean Louis enjoying the games.

But the fisherman had work to do, so I climbed into the fishing boat and we moved off to pull in some pots. Jean Louis obviously knew the boat and what to expect. The water was beautifully clear and we watched her diving excitedly round each pot as it was hauled to the surface. The fisherman dispatched a conger eel that was in one of his pots by a knife-cut across the back of the neck. The crabs were put into a box. The catch from the first string of pots was good, and the pots were rebaited and put down again.

Then we moved off to another location. Jean Louis followed until we moved over the invisible boundary line. Then she left us. So the next string of pots was hauled from the water without the distraction of a dolphin.

The third and final string of pots was, however, within Jean Louis' territorial limits, and she joined us again. When he had finished pulling up his pots, the fisherman produced a large bottle of red wine from which we all took liberal libations to celebrate. The fisherman because he had a good catch; and Peter and I because we both looked forward to returning to make a film.

· 4 ·

Percy Reappears

I had no news of Percy during the winter of 1982–3, and wondered if he had swum away from Cornwall never to return. However, just before I left for France on the reconnaissance trip with Peter Gillbe I had a letter from Judy Holborn informing me that there had been a week of glorious weather from 19 to 25 June, and that several local fishermen had seen Percy around Godrevy Island. At the weekend Bob had taken Judy and some friends to the island in his inflatable to see if they could locate the dolphin. They left at high tide, 5 p.m., in perfect conditions. Near Godrevy they met a fisherman who had seen the dolphin, who was now down by Fisherman's Cove. Bob motored on to the cove, but found only some friendly seals. Everyone was pleased to see the seals, but disappointed that Percy was not there.

Then, suddenly, as Bob was setting a course back to Portreath, a dolphin leapt high out of the water within inches of the boat. Judy shrieked with surprise and delight. After cruising around for a short time, with the dolphin swimming close by, Bob turned off the engine. Percy, seeming really to enjoy being near the inflatable and its excited occupants, came so close that Bob just managed to touch his head. The water was exceptionally clear and Bob wished he had taken his wetsuit. When they set off again the dolphin followed the inflatable all the way back to Portreath. Judy noted that Percy had many marks and scars, including one that looked like a bullet wound about half-way along the right-hand side of his body when seen from the front. They left the dolphin playing joyfully among some buoys and lines in the bay in front of Beach House.

Bob was delighted to make contact with Percy again after his winter-long disappearance, and planned to go out every evening the following week. But the weather broke, and in her letter, dated 26 June, Judy said it was now too rough to go out to sea.

Two weeks had elapsed since then, and the weather had turned fine again. Despite the pleasure I had derived from visiting Jean Louis in Brittany I was keen to renew my acquaintance with Percy if I could. I had two clear days between lecture engagements immediately after my return to Gatwick and decided to use them for a trip to Cornwall. One of my commitments was a lecture at a school in Sussex on 11 July, in which I included the film I had made about Donald in St Ives. Seeing the film brought back into sharp focus that long, hot summer of 1976, and fond memories of the remarkable friendship that had developed between myself and the wild dolphin. However, I was not the only person to feel a tremendous affection for Donald. Even a brief sighting of him was often the highlight of a vacation for many holiday-makers, who could still, years later, vividly recall the details.

It never ceased to amaze me how the paths of such people seemed to cross mine. A typical example was that of Mrs Luxford, the landlady of the house in Eastergate in Sussex where I found bed-and-breakfast accommodation following my film/lecture presentation. She told me how thrilled she had been with her brief sighting of Donald. I have to admit that I much prefer the exchange of appropriate goods and services as payment to the exchange of money, as it puts the transaction on a much more personal basis. The thought of the peripatetic Laurie Lee, author of *Cider with Rosie*, earning his supper by playing a tune on his fiddle appeals to me. Paying Mrs Luxford for my accommodation with a signed copy of my book on Donald set me in a good mood. And I was looking forward to my journey to Portreath, enjoying the spice of being unable to predict the outcome.

The ocean is a big place. With just two friendly wild dolphins in the entire world the statistical chance of a meeting in the open sea with both of them within a few days is extremely remote. Even if Percy was in Cornwall one day he could move away at any time, turning up off the coast of Wales, France, or even Spain.

Tuesday, 12 July, was the hottest July day since the heatwave of 1976, during which I had successfully set out to find and film Donald. Now I was going back to Cornwall in remarkably similar circumstances to find Percy. As I drove along the familiar roads to the West Country I still had the film images fresh in my mind, and I wondered if Percy was related to Donald in any way. Had he inherited from Donald the characteristic of seeking human company instead of that of his fellow dolphins? If so, it would seem to be a self-eliminating gene, for unless he mated there would be no more solitary friendly dolphins to carry on the line.

I stopped at the Jamaica Inn on Bodmin Moor for afternoon tea. It was sultry and still. The tar on the road was melting with the heat, and I joined the jostling crowd of tourists, most of whom wanted long, cool drinks. The scene could not have contrasted more with the images of cold, fog and desolation conjured up in Daphne du Maurier's book. I had decided to take a leisurely journey to Portreath, planning to spend the following day gathering information and, depending upon the outcome, to plan for a future return trip. As I approached Portreath and got my first glimpse of the sea I knew immediately that conditions were perfect. Bob would certainly have been out looking for Percy. Had he managed to locate the dolphin again? I wondered what the latest news would be.

I pulled into the drive at Beach House in Portreath at 5.10 p.m. Judy was in the garden. She was very excited about the behaviour of Percy and said that he had been seen again off Godrevy Island. Then she said that a group from the Harrow Film School had come down to film the dolphin and was due to leave the harbour at 5.30 p.m. with Alan Vine. Judy was as helpful as ever and, being a born organiser, immediately telephoned the fisherman to ask him if he would take another passenger.

Alan Vine lived in a large rambling house on top of the hill just a few hundred yards from Smugglers' Cove. He suggested I walk up to the house so that he could give me a lift to the harbour, as he would be leaving very shortly. Within a few moments of my arrival in Portreath I was preparing to go to sea.

Alan was a big man with fair hair and a bushy beard. Unlike most fishermen, he had first-hand experience of life under the sea because he was also a diver. He had a very cheerful disposition, and I remembered the story about one of his encounters with Percy the previous year. I also recognised him as one of the fishermen I had spoken to when I first went out to search for the dolphin with Keith Pope. His boat was of unusual design, short and stubby, with a sealed hull which meant that it was virtually unsinkable. However, even in a moderate sea, water rushed in through the gaps at the bottom of the gunwales on one side, flowed across the deck and then poured out through the other side as the boat rolled. Alan was accustomed to its incessant rolling motion, but for land lubbers without sea legs, into which category the group from the Harrow Film School had to be placed, it was less comfortable. Fortunately the sea was kind to them on their first journey aboard the *Tar dor Moor* (named, Alan told me, in the Cornish for 'Sea Dawn').

In addition to the Harrow group there were two divers on the small boat. Both were heavily bearded, and both were red-faced when their heads popped through the tight neck-seals of the drysuits they were putting on when we climbed aboard. As we journeyed towards Godrevy Island in search of Percy I chatted to one of them, John Bishop. He told me he had first met Percy during a routine dive from the *Tar dor Moor*, on 9 June, 1982. John had dived close to Portreath on a wreck called the *Escurial*. After attaching a line, prior to commencing a salvaging dive for non-ferrous metal, and returning to the surface, the skipper, Alan Vine, had asked him if he had seen the huge grey fish that was swimming nearby. John got out of the sea as quickly as he could, knowing that sharks were occasionally found in the area, and refused to go back in until he knew what the big fish was. Alan left the wreck site and began to haul in a string of lobster pots. He was interrupted by a dolphin, which appeared on the bow and escorted the boat back to the wreck site. 'I still wasn't over-happy with it being there – because of its size,' he continued. 'Eventually I was persuaded to go over the side and went to the bottom. I could just see the dolphin swimming on the edge of visibility, not quite visible but I knew he was there. I carried on with what I had to do and never saw any more of him after that.'

John recorded his dives in a diary and was therefore able to recall what he'd done. I in return recorded what he said on my tape-recorder:

> I went out three days later with another diver – I wasn't very brave – but the dolphin never turned up.
>
> Two weeks later we were again on the *Escurial*. This time I decided that if he was going to be there I was going to get him on film. As soon as we got to the bottom he was swimming around us twenty to thirty feet away. Unfortunately on that dive the boat wasn't staying with us. They were off working while we were left on the bottom. As the boat went off, so did the dolphin. We had high hopes of him coming back when the boat returned to pick us up. But unfortunately the boat broke down and never came back. So we never saw him again that day. We swam back to shore and the boat was towed in later.

John was anxious that records of sighting of Percy should be accurate. He informed me that the first ever divers to meet Percy were from Wales. In later correspondence with one of them I was able to pinpoint the date precisely from his log book. It was 17 April, 1982. Here is how Paul Hearne from Bridgend described in a letter his meeting with the dolphin.

It was about one o'clock in the afternoon when we set out in our inflatable from Portreath Harbour. We headed right out of the harbour towards two large rocks standing out of the sea. Just as we were at the rocks a dolphin broke surface on the starboard side. The dolphin stayed around the bow of the inflatable while myself and Steve put on our cylinders and fins (about ten seconds in the circumstances). We entered the sea for a dive of twenty-five minutes at eighteen metres. We did not see the dolphin when we were in the sea, but while Chris was motoring around in the inflatable the dolphin stayed with him all the time.

Steve and I finished the dive and got into the inflatable, but the dolphin had just gone out of sight. When we were all safely in the inflatable the dolphin appeared immediately and stayed with us as we motored off for about five minutes, and then it disappeared again.

It seemed to me that the dolphin was wary of divers in the water but didn't mind us at all if we stayed in the boat.

This was valuable information to me because the dolphin's subsequent behaviour showed a progression of boldness and friendship towards humans in the sea.

There was no sign of the dolphin, and we continued our conversation as the *Tar dor Moor* progressed towards Godrevy Island. 'What are your feelings about the dolphin when you dive with him? Do you feel he's like a fish?' I asked John.

'He's definitely not a fish,' came the reply. 'He's got a personality. He's almost like a person, but not quite. Sort of superhuman person. He can swim better than I can, he can dive better than I can and I think he senses things better than I can.'

'Have you ever felt scared of him apart from the first time when you didn't know him?' I asked.

'Since I've actually seen him in plain view, no. No fear whatsoever. I've been very close to him and made a move towards him and tried to get hold of one of his fins, but he's very nervous and moves his fin away.'

I also spoke to the student from Harrow who had come aboard clutching a 16mm Bolex cine-camera. He told me that he wanted to make a film about dolphins as part of his studies. Instead of taking the easy option and going to a dolphinarium he had chosen to make the trip to Portreath on the merest chance he might be able to film a wild dolphin it its natural environment. Having no money, he had hitch-hiked from London, the journey taking two days. When he arrived he asked Judy if he could camp on her lawn. Judy, generous as ever, had given him a bed in the house free of charge. She had also contacted Alan Vine and persuaded him to take the impoverished future David Lean out for a free trip on the fishing boat.

As we approached Godrevy Island chatty conversation ceased. All eyes and minds were concentrated on finding the dolphin. The air was hazy with a light high-summer mist and the lighthouse on Godrevy Island stood silhouetted against a pale blue-grey sky.

'Here he comes!' shouted John Bishop.

We all turned to watch Percy racing towards us. He dived under the boat and weaved from side to side in front of the bows. The young cameraman immediately went into action, pointing his camera directly downwards to capture the dolphin's graceful, curving sweeps. As he did so, the character of the water abruptly changed to a turbid misty-grey. I knew this would make editing the film very difficult, and when I pointed this out to the skipper he informed me that we had come up to what he called the 'Red River', the outlet of a river carrying sediment down from the mines to pollute the sea close to Godrevy Island.

'See if you can entice the dolphin back towards Portreath where the water is clearer,' suggested John, who was keen to get in the water. But Alan had already decided on the same course of action. With Percy still gambolling in the bows, we moved out of the dirty water and headed north-east. Alan, who had been smiling ever since we left harbour, had an even bigger grin on his broad, friendly face. He had a dolphin on the bows and a jubilant crowd aboard. He was a happy man.

As the divers made their final preparations to dive, Alan switched the engine into neutral and left his tiny wheelhouse. The big fisherman chatted in a deep Cornish accent to the dolphin, who came alongside and looked up at the bearded face that swayed back and forth with the rocking boat.

The two divers jumped overboard, John clutching his 8mm cine-camera. He and his companion vented the air from their suits and turned head downwards, their fins raised briefly out of the water before sliding smoothly beneath the surface. I watched them descend, and could clearly see Percy's white belly as he too went head-first towards the sea bed. At the same time the cameraman came back to the wheelhouse to change the film in his camera. I was about to give him a hand when I noticed John surface rapidly. A split second later there was a whoosh alongside him and Percy hurtled out of the sea. The dolphin arched over John's head and crashed back into the sea, showering me and my land camera with water. A few seconds later Percy leapt again, then again.

By the time the cameraman had reloaded with film, only John's head was still visible on the surface. He had deliber-ately rushed up and the dolphin had followed him. When the camera was reloaded we asked him for a repeat performance, which he obligingly gave us, several times. But Percy had spent his energy and cruised around slowly, apparently enjoying watching John attempting to launch himself into space.

John Bishop stayed in the water for nearly two hours playing with Percy, during which time Bob and Judy Holborn arrived in their inflatable with three passengers aboard. They pulled alongside and then did some sweeps around us, but in contrast to the conclusions Keith Pope and I had come to the previous year, on this occasion Percy was much more interested in what was happening on the sea bed than on the surface.

We tried to entice Percy back to Portreath. Three times we went back through the rough water at Navax Point. Three times Percy followed us through the tidal race and then turned back to Godrevy. He had fixed his boundary line for the day and wasn't prepared to go any further – no matter how tempting we made it by motoring from side to side with the inflatable or the fishing boat. So we steamed back to Portreath and tied up at 10 p.m., twenty minutes before the harbour dried out at low water.

As a fisherman, Alan's life was dictated by the weather and the tides. His visit to Godrevy had been a pleasure trip to see the dolphin. Tomorrow he would have to work. As we unloaded the diving equipment he told me he would be back in the harbour at 5.30 the following morning.

I slept with the window wide open that night and awoke at precisely 5.30 a.m. Judy had thoughtfully left beside the bed all the ingredients, including a jug of fresh milk, for me to make a cup of tea, so I sat by the window, sipping my tea and watching the sun rise, blood-orange red, over the harbour. As it climbed above the horizon it created a shimmering crimson pathway across the bay. At 6 a.m. I heard the sound of an engine and the *Tar dor Moor* appeared from the harbour entrance. 'Tar dor Moor', 'Tar dor Moor', 'Sea Dawn' ... what an appropriate name, I thought, as I watched the small vessel piled high with lobster pots move slowly across the sun-dappled sea. In my mind I could see Alan smiling to himself and wondering if he would have a dolphin for company as he worked his pots. He knew he would have to be back by 10.30, before the harbour dried out at low water if he were not to remain at sea all day. He had agreed to take me out at 6 p.m., on the next rising tide.

My morning was spent sitting on the lawn watching a

pied wagtail run back and forth, its tail bobbing up and down like a fast metronome. Bob came out, commented 'It's hell in paradise,' and went back indoors smiling. The beach was empty. I listened to the music of the ocean. Then a solitary jogger trotted along the high-water line.

During the morning the beach at Portreath became completely covered with happy human bodies. Tiny tots toddled into the edge of the sea, watched by their parents, while teenagers rushed, splashing and shrieking through the oncoming water, to throw themselves into the walls of advancing waves.

As the beach filled, I climbed the steep cliff path to the west of Beach House. Underfoot, wild flowers blossomed in profusion. Lilac-blue vetch, yellow birdsfoot trefoil (or eggs and bacon as it is sometimes called) and reddish-purple bretony formed a springy cushion for me to walk upon. Soon the high-pitched shrieks of children playing on the beach fell behind me and were replaced by the cries of gulls. The higher I climbed the better I could see down into the sea. Never before had I seen the water so clear off the north Cornish coast. Patches of aquamarine sand surrounded undersea islands covered with dark green kelp. Through my binoculars I scanned Gull Rock and could see the black silhouettes of cormorants, their wings outstretched to dry in the sun, standing like a row of crucifixes against the sparkling blue backdrop of the sea. The unmatched beauty of the scene slowly invaded my body until I felt I was on the edge of a new universe. I moved my gaze downwards. At the foot of the cliffs the pale brown sand of the beaches, unveiled at low water, were unmarked by human footprints. Two seals surfaced beside a rock and looked quizzically at the squawking gulls. Then they sank smoothly into the depths and I watched their grey bodies, mottled with black spots, gliding effortlessly through the kelp-covered canyons of their undersea world. A tiny fishing boat chugged very quietly into the picture and moved across the big screen. The far distant horizon melted into the sky. The sea and air went on for ever. Godrevy

Island with its lighthouse stood in the sea like a cake with a solitary candle.

Then, in the midst of all the beauty, I spotted a tiny cameo of tragedy close to the base of the cliff. An injured black-backed gull was floating on its back in the water with its wings partly outstretched, waving its webbed feet in the air, its head occasionally arching back under the water. Its struggles were useless. The bird would not survive, and I could do nothing to help it for it was hundreds of feet below me. I climbed higher until I reached the edge of the deep indentation in the cliffs known locally as Ralph's Cupboard. I had entered the tiny enclosed cove from the sea the previous year. It was equally impressive from above as from below. I found a ledge close to the edge and was lulled into a doze by the warmth of the sun and the sound of the sea. One day I would write a fictional story about this magic place.

While I lazed on the cliff-top, Bob Holborn was out in his inflatable. He didn't see Percy, but he did catch some mackerel which we cooked on a barbecue on the lawn before setting out for the harbour with the cameraman from Harrow. This time we knew what to expect. I had my diving gear at the ready. All the cameras were carefully prepared for immediate action when we met Percy again. When the *Tar dor Moor* left the harbour at Portreath for the second time, on the second rising tide of the day, at 6.15 p.m., conditions were absolutely perfect. 'We didn't have a single day with underwater visibility like this last year,' remarked Alan as I chatted to him on the way to Godrevy Island. The sea was smooth, so for once the *Tar dor Moor* didn't roll at all.

We chugged alongside a fishing boat near the island.

'Have you seen the dolphin?' Alan called out.

'We've only just arrived. No we haven't,' came the reply.

'Some fishermen say they've seen him at St Ives Island,' said Alan.

'Let's head on there, then,' I suggested.

We continued our journey westwards across the glassy

sea towards St Ives Island, which slowly took shape out of the haze. Now we were in precisely the territory where I had filmed Donald. The scene was one of great tranquillity. A few fishing vessels moved like toy boats on pink-tinted water, across which rolled the muffled sounds of chugging engines and squawking seagulls blended with the distant rumble of holiday-makers on the shore and the barely perceptible murmur of waves on the beach.

We caught some mackerel and headed back towards Godrevy Island. The light started to fade quickly as the sun, getting progressively dimmer, crept closer to the horizon. A small fishing boat headed our way.

'Have you seen the dolphin?'

'Yes, he's over on the Stones,' came the reply.

The Stones form the rocky top of a treacherous reef extending seawards from Godrevy Island and are a danger to shipping, the main reason for the existence of the lighthouse. At low water some of the rocks that constitute the Stones are exposed. But at high water the same rocks are hidden just beneath the surface, to the destruction of many ships. A further hazard is constituted by the strong currents that rip between the submerged rocks. I thought Alan would head back for Portreath. But instead he turned his boat north and, with the sun sliding silently into the sea, we moved towards the buoy marking the outermost limit of the Stones.

Suddenly, a dolphin rushed past our bows as if to deflect us. We looked over the side to where he had come from and saw, fifteen feet away, a pyramid of rock rising to within a few inches of the surface. The young man acting as crew looked worried and shouted to Alan, 'If we had hit that rock hidden just below the surface we could have sunk.'

'I reckon Percy came to warn us,' replied the skipper, as he steered well clear of the hazard.

We enjoyed Percy's company for a few minutes. There were no spectacular leaps. He swam alongside and raised his head out of the water to look at us, then circled the boat several times and was gone.

The sea and the sky were merging into a deepening grey-orange cloth. There were no other colours, just black silhouettes. Even the seagulls that flew overhead were black, as were their reflections on the water. It was a strange, magical world, one of absolute peace and tranquillity.

We steered back towards Portreath and the sky turned steadily darker. The three lights on the road to the Royal Airforce Station above Portreath twinkled.

'I see Mother's remembered to put the candles in the jars to guide us home,' joked the crew member. 'We tell the visitors that, they believe anything,' he added, laughing.

A tiny crescent moon brightened in the sky. The sea was full of phosphorescence. It was quite dark when we eventually slipped into the harbour at Portreath, at 11 p.m.

On our return to Beach House we found a note telling us to help ourselves to tea. As an afterthought there was a P.S. which read as follows:

Hope you found him – we couldn't find you – were at Godrevy Lighthouse from 8.15 to 9 and spent all that time with 'him'. Fantastic display. Tell you tomorrow.

Jude

Over breakfast the next morning Judy explained that they had come out to look for us, but had instead found Percy by Godrevy Island. The dolphin came up and winked at Susan on the bows of the inflatable before doing a series of sensational jumps. I could imagine the shrieks of delight. Bob reported that the dolphin came up under his inflatable when it was under way and lifted it several times.

'If I were a dolphin I'd live on the Stones,' he said. 'A dolphin's paradise.'

We had our breakfast on the lawn outside Beach House. As Bob and Judy recounted their adventure, a solitary seal cruised slowly past, about ten yards off-shore. Again, conditions were absolutely perfect. The sea was flat calm

4 *Above left*: I recognised the Pakistani fisherman painted on
the side of the Pelletiers' vehicle.
5 *Above right*: Stained-glass window in the author's front door
depicting Jean Louis under-water; it was designed by
Lynne Emmerson.
6 Jean Louis over the kelp forest.

7 Percy would often move a boat after lifting the anchor.

and the water was so clear we could see the seal swimming under-water. But I had to leave. That evening I had to give a film show in London and then get ready to go to France to make a film about Jean Louis.

· 5 ·

Assignment Adventure

Assignment Adventure was the title of the television series my film about Jean Louis would appear in, and the making of the film certainly turned out to be an adventurous assignment. It took me into the sea in conditions far more severe than I had ever attempted before, and which I would previously have described as suicidal. In addition to extending my own ability to survive in, and indeed to enjoy diving in, very rough water, I made a positive step forward in my understanding of the dolphin psyche. Although I didn't realise at the time, the two advances were closely linked.

The filming adventure began on Thursday, 21 July, 1983, when, my car packed with cameras, lighting equipment and diving gear, I headed south to meet Peter Gillbe in London. London was roasting hot, and the cool, air-conditioned atmosphere in Peter's office contrasted with the hot, smelly traffic outside. I loaded even more packages into my car before finally setting out in the sweltering sun for Cornwall. My destination was James Wharram's base in Devoran, near Truro.

The excitement of going on a filming venture had already infected the Dolphin Link headquarters, and when I arrived at 9.15 p.m. Ruth Wharram and Sarah King rushed out and flung their arms round me in greeting. Part of James Wharram's philosophy is that clothes are an encumbrance that should be discarded whenever possible. As a result it is quite usual to find his (numercially) female-dominated household full of unclothed or partly clothed people. The evening I arrived was no exception. Inside the house on the

66

polished wooden floor lay a naked lady in the prone position. It was Carola Hepp, a girl I had last seen when visiting Wade Doak in New Zealand. Hanneke Boon, wearing only a sarong skirt, was bending over the recumbent body and applying pressure to different parts with her fingers. A cheerful face with blue eyes looked up at me. Carola explained that wielding a hatchet to clear some of the scrub-covered ground around the Dolphin Link Centre had made her back ache. Hanneke was attempting to relieve the pain. Eventually Carola got up, claimed that most of the pain had gone, and pulled on a loose dress. She then hurried away and returned with a painting done on linen which showed a girl and a dolphin swimming together, one visible through the other. She said that she was trying to depict the two swimming together as they might be seen by another dolphin, with a combination of sonic and visual images overlapping.

Various other youngsters materialised and soon the room was full of excited people all keen to be involved with dolphins and to hear about the project in Brittany. First, however, I had to hear about their encounters with Percy the previous Sunday. The meeting with the local friendly dolphin gave them all a tremendous fillip. It was just the kind of stimulus the filming project needed to get it off to a good start, especially as at this point James dropped his first bombshell.

'You realise, Horace, that you are asking me to sail into one of the most dangerous places in the world, don't you?' he asked, rhetorically.

We were joined by Eric, a huge young Frenchman who spoke a little English and had sailed through the area in Brittany we were about to visit. He said that nobody should sail around La Baie des Trépassés, which he translated into English as the Bay of Tragedies. We pondered over charts and accounts of voyages in the area which we culled from books in James's extensive library. It appeared that on both sides of the bay there were extremely strong currents, some of which ran counter to one another with a speed of five knots. There were also many shoals and submerged reefs in the area. The vessel we were to use for the expedition, which had been designed and built by James Wharram, was a Polynesian-style sailing catamaran with an overall length of fifty-one feet. The maximum speed the *Teheni* could achieve with its auxiliary engine as the sole source of propulsion was six knots. This left only a very small leeway of safety in such strong currents. If a westerly gale blew there would be no escape, and the vessel could easily be wrecked.

James then pointed out another difficulty. The ship's papers had been lost. Apparently when the *Teheni* had been sailed to the West Indies by one of the joint-owners the paperwork had been misplaced and nobody had thought to renew it. The French were extremely difficult under such circumstances and in the Mediterranean had recently impounded a Zodiac inflatable from England because the appropriate papers were not available. From what James said, I deduced that in most parts of the world officials seldom asked for papers. As we talked I could see flashes of lightning cutting patterns into the black sky. I hoped the break in the weather was not some ominous portent.

When I eventually went to bed that night it seemed uncertain that the *Teheni* would actually be able to make it to La Baie des Trépassés. I lay on my mattress on the floor watching through the bamboo blind clouds race past the moon. But soon the problem was lost in the unconsciousness of sleep. It had been a long day and it was now well past midnight.

I have often found that problems that seem unsolvable when I am tired are much easier to resolve after a good night's sleep. The following morning we reviewed the situation. James was very keen to go to Brittany, and we discussed how, if necessary, we could lash an inflatable to the side of the *Teheni* to give the catamaran extra power through the tidal races. We also decided that the way to tackle the navigational hazards in the bay would be to find somebody locally who knew these waters. James would sail to France and find a safe anchorage in Brittany. With local knowledge he could then assess the possibilities of taking the *Teheni* to La Baie des Trépassés on a daily basis. So it was with optimism that I left Devoran in a downpour of rain to head back towards Plymouth, where I would meet the rest of the film crew who were coming out from London. Our plan of campaign was that the film crew would sail to Brittany on the Plymouth to Roscoff ferry. They would take a Humber inflatable with an engine and could therefore start filming immediately. James would sail the *Teheni* across to France when he had sorted out the papers and the weather conditions were favourable.

The man in charge of the above-water camera team was Paul Berriff, a Humberside coastguard. In addition to the mountain of cameras and recording gear, he took to France an inshore rescue boat, towed behind his Volvo. I had known the underwater cameraman, Peter Scoones, for many years, but had never worked with him before. His assistant, Georgie Douwma, was a petite Dutch lady. We had decided to use the Hôtel de la Ville d'Ys as our base, but as it was fully booked the film crew were dispersed at various hotels in Audierne and the surrounding countryside. The filming operations themselves were to be centred on the tiny harbour near Dolphin Rock, and it was agreed that we would all rendezvous there mid-morning on the first day of filming, Saturday, 23 July.

The last words James Wharram said to me as I left Devoran were that it was very dangerous to be in La Baie des Trépassés with an onshore westerly wind, which was exactly what was blowing – and strongly – when I arrived to start filming. The sea in the region of the rock around which we hoped to film Jean Louis was a seething mass of white foam. Could we get the catamaran into La Baie des Trépassés? Could we even make a film, I wondered. We had to make a start.

As we began unpacking the Humber inflatable and its engine, I noticed a very attractive young woman climbing up the steep cliff path towards the rocky platform where we were assembling our inflatable. She carried a very large single fin with two foot-shoes in it. It was similar in design to one used by Wade Doak in his Project Interlock, for which he had attempted to make an underwater swimmer as dolphin-like as possible. Wade had dressed his wife, Jan, in a wetsuit in which her legs were encased in a single tube. Both feet were attached to a single fin which she moved up and down in the so-called dolphin stroke. During a visit to New Zealand I had examined the suit and the fin, and we had gone for a single sail on Wade's Wharram-designed catamaran. We failed to find any dolphins on that occasion, so I did not see the suit and fins in action, but Wade assured me that once a person mastered the technique of using the monofin it was an extremely efficient method of propulsion, and that for long-distance swimming it was less tiring to use than the conventional method of doing crawl using two fins. Naturally, I was intrigued to see another person with a monofin. As the girl carrying it climbed the cliff a young man with a black moustache descended the path to meet her. They engaged in serious conversation and looked at the sea. Although I couldn't hear what they were saying, I could read body language. They discussed the sea conditions, decided it was too rough to go into the water, and abandoned whatever it was they proposed to do.

I decided to introduce myself and see if I could find out what they were up to. The man's English was better than my French, and we conducted our conversation in a stilted mixture of both languages. His name was François Pelletier and he told me he was there to make a fictional film about Jean Louis in which the beautiful young lady carrying the monofin was to star.

To succeed in the film-making business it is essential to be single-minded. The lengths to which film crews will go in order to get footage is legendary. To have two rival film crews from different countries competing for the attention of a solitary wild dolphin would make filming tricky, to say the least. The complete unpredictability of the weather and the desire of both crews to be in the water when the underwater visibility was good were additional ingredients in a recipe for confrontation which I was anxious to avoid. François Pelletier was also sensitive to the implications of this situation, so both of us were diplomatically friendly towards one another. Our underwater cine-cameras had not been assembled, and François said conditions were not good enough for him to shoot film. When I expressed my desire to renew my acquaintance with Jean Louis, François suggested that despite the poor conditions we should go for a dive together to find the dolphin. I readily agreed.

We both kitted up in our wetsuits and aqualungs. Just as we were about to set off for the scramble down the cliffs, a lady who was obviously very pregnant appeared on the scene pushing a baby buggy in which sat a delightful young child. It was Catherine Pelletier, wife of François. I was introduced to her and her smiling daughter Delphine, whose name was derived from the Latin name of the Common dolphin, *Delphinus delphis*, which frequents the Mediterranean and occurs in many of the ancient legends. I immediately fell in love with Delphine – not because of her name but because I adore young children. Before we departed for our dive I accepted an invitation to pay the Pelletiers a visit that evening. With such a charming family I was hopeful that we could resolve any clash of interest.

I apprised Peter Gillbe of the situation and left him still working on the inflatable while I went for a dive. The water was grey, and numerous sand eels wriggled through the underwater mist. Jean Louis did not honour us with her presence, even when François descended and tapped his cylinder with his knife. So we headed towards Dolphin Rock. As we swam along a rope covered in green algae came into my vision. I grabbed it and pulled it downwards, and an aluminium buoy bobbed into view. Recognising it from my earlier visit in May, I took my knife from its scabbard and hammered the hollow sphere with the heavy handle. As I slid the knife back into the sheath on my leg, a smiling dolphin's face appeared out of the underwater haze and silently disappeared again. We moved closer towards Dolphin Rock, feeling the swirl from the rough water and keeping an eye out for the occasional clouds of tiny white bubbles. It was a dangerous zone to move into and we kept well clear. Jean Louis swam around us and passed very close several times, but our glimpses of her were short-lived because of the poor visibility.

The important thing was that I had re-established contact with Jean Louis. My plan was to get into the water with her as often as I could, not just when conditions for filming were good. In that way I hoped she would not regard me as one of the many casual visitors who came to Dolphin Rock, but as a friendly familiar alien whose presence did not threaten her in any way. Indeed, I hoped that eventually we could build an interspecies bond that would go beyond that of, say, a sheepdog and his master. When we got to that stage I could progress towards an even more significant partnership. I had created the opportunity and I now had the resources I needed – but only for two weeks, or at the most three weeks. Could I make a breakthrough in that relatively short space of time? In hindsight I realise I was perhaps over-optimistic, and certainly presumptuous from the dolphin's point of view. However, I had made a good start by establishing contact with Jean Louis on the first morning of my return to the Bay of Lost Souls.

Conflict between the two film crews was still possible, but I felt it could be averted if I applied the lessons I had learnt during and after my experiences in the competitive commercial world of research, development and marketing of new drugs. It was based on the premise that even in a competitive situation there is room for everybody, and that deceit in business creates many more problems than it resolves. Thus when I set off to find the Pelletiers that evening I resolved to tell them quite openly why I had come to Brittany and what I hoped to achieve, and to ask for their cooperation.

I had no difficulty finding them. They were snugly

pitched in the corner of a field surrounded by bracken, partly protected from the wind coming from the west which carried with it a spray of fine rain. Beside their tent was a white van, on the side of which a picture showed a be-turbaned Asian holding in his arms an Indus River dolphin, *Plantanista indi*. I recognised the man as the fisherman upon whose primitive, raft-like boat I had slept and sailed when I paid a memorable visit to the Indus River in Pakistan, in search of the rare blind river dolphins. It seemed there was a good deal of common ground between François Pelletier and myself.

Despite certain language difficulties, it very soon became apparent that François was not in Brittany simply to exploit a unique situation. He and his wife were true dolphin enthusiasts, prepared to sacrifice a great deal in order to pursue their love of and commitment to dolphins. The film François was making was quite different to mine, a fantasy. We agreed that to have two camera crews in the water at the same time must be avoided at all costs, and that we would work out a rough time-table for filming on a daily basis. From the start Peter Gillbe agreed with my approach. He said he felt very sympathetic towards François Pelletier, who was obviously working on a very small budget, and that we should cooperate with the small French film team.

Part of the agreement with the Pelletiers was that we would film under-water in the mornings and late afternoons, leaving the middle of the day for them. We accordingly went to start filming the next morning at 9.30 a.m. Our star, however, declined to appear at such an early hour. After twenty minutes of fruitless searching I dived down beneath the kelp and found two stones which I banged together. I could hear the sounds penetrating the water like pistol shots, but even these failed to attract Jean Louis. After discussing the situation with Peter on the surface, I descended to the kelp once again, and it was then that Jean Louis responded to my signal. Thus the very first sequence filmed showed my legs waving above the kelp forest with a dolphin looking quizzically at them. I was quite unaware that Jean Louis had arrived, and by the time I emerged she was gone. That is very often how events turn out in underwater film-making, with the spectator and the cameraman seeing more of the game than the participant. When Peter was shooting the sequence he had no idea if it would fit into the story we would eventually tell, or whether, like so many other sequences he shot, it would end up on the cutting-room floor.

The water was still cloudy, and when Jean Louis came into view she gave me the eerie impression of a space ship carrying an alien intelligence from another world. I was interested to discover to what extent dolphins register 'aesthetic' experiences through their sensory perceptions, and to that end I tried several simple experiments. I pulled down a buoy and let it rise erratically to the surface. Jean Louis did not seem particularly interested. I also cut off a piece of kelp and waved it for her benefit. To me, the curves it formed as it wafted to and fro were graceful and artistic. The dolphin has a fixed jawline set in a permanent smile, so I could not read her face as I can that of a human, who expresses joy or sadness by the upturn or downturn of the lips. And though the eyes of a dolphin are expressive, I could not detect that minute change in appearance which in humans is often the sole indicator of inner emotions. I honestly couldn't tell what she was thinking.

There were many sources of alternative diving activities to attract the dolphin's attention while we were underwater attempting to film her. At times Jean Louis would disappear for five minutes or more before coming back. We didn't realise just how many diversions there were until we surfaced. It was a hot, sunny Sunday, and the tiny harbour was seething with divers of different nationalities, including Dutch, German, French and English. Jean Louis was certainly a Euro-dolphin.

Peter Gillbe suggested that if I wanted to establish a strong relationship with Jean Louis I should be the first person she met in the morning and the last she saw in the evening. This seemed a good idea, so the next morning I went to the little harbour before breakfast. Conditions were perfect, a slight wind blowing from the land and the water flat calm. Putting on my wetsuit and snorkelling equipment, I descended the steep slipway and slid very gently into the water. The visibility was far better than I had ever seen it before around the stone steps at the bottom of the slipway. I could see every detail of the submerged stonework, while the seaweeds, illuminated by the soft morning light, transformed the scenery just beneath the surface into a lush and beautiful underwater garden.

The only other people in the harbour were two fishermen out in a boat. As I snorkelled slowly away from the shore I thought I would have Jean Louis' attention entirely to myself. I had picked two stones out of the bank where I parked my car, and now I clapped them together, expecting to see her face appear at any moment. It didn't. I swam right round Dolphin Rock and back to our boat, which was on a mooring in the bay. Still Jean Louis did not appear. Even when I climbed into the inflatable, started the engine and set off on a tour of the bay I could not find her. What had happened? Had I been exceptionally lucky the previous day?

I went and had some breakfast at the hotel, returning eventually at 10.30 to the jetty, where a group of divers was assembling. A couple of them were already in the water, and we looked expectantly at the surface, but could see no characteristic dorsal fin. Then, two minutes later, a cry went up and there below us was a grey back topped by a dark grey recurved fin. Jean Louis had arrived. She immediately went to the divers and circled around them. After about ten minutes she vanished.

Our diving team kitted up. Having decided that she appeared to be more interested when divers moved quickly through the water, I decided not to take my aqualung into the boat and wore just my fins, mask and snorkel. With Georgie Douwma handling the boat we went out beyond Dolphin Rock, and within a few moments were being trailed by the dolphin. Peter and I immediately jumped overboard. It was delightful not to have the encumbrance of an aqualung, but to swim swiftly through the water with the dolphin. Peter stayed quietly filming while I snorkel-dived time and time again, accompanied by Jean Louis, who often swam with her eye just a few inches from my face. She would watch me intently and then, with a couple of flicks of her tail, accelerate away.

Georgie circled in the inflatable. When she suddenly accelerated Jean Louis hurtled away from me. A few seconds later I saw the dolphin rise six feet out of the water in a magnificent leap as she followed the speeding boat. Then she came back to us, remained in the water with her head downwards, and quivered. I could see her stomach contracting. It was almost as if she was in a spasm after her energetic leap. Then she zoomed away into the clear grey water. I tried swimming dolphin stroke and she seemed to enjoy that.

We played with Jean Louis for some time and then were joined by a group of canoeists, friends of Andy Crofts, who had first alerted me to the presence of Jean Louis in France. We had a marvellous time together in the water. One of them did a barrel-roll and the dolphin went up and peered into his submerged face very intently. It was a comical sight – a canoeist wearing a lifejacket and a crash helmet, upside-down in the water, with a dolphin peering into his face from a few inches away. Eventually he rolled back into an upright position and we agreed this would make a good sequence for the film. We chatted as we bobbed around on the water, and one of the group told me that he had been to see Percy just a few days before. They had visited Judy and Bob, got the directions of Percy's location from them and paddled out. Apparently the current had been strong and the underwater visibility not very good, but they had had an encounter with the Cornish dolphin. Now, just a few days later, they were in France enjoying the company of Percy's French cousin.

Eventually we returned to the shore, so that François Pelletier could keep his mid-day appointment with Jean

Louis without the distraction of our film crew. Happy with the result of our morning's filming, we headed back to the hotel for a protracted lunch.

Two hours later we were back at the port, but we found the scene utterly transformed. White water reared up the cliff face on the far side of the bay. The sky was grey. The wind was strengthening and blowing in straight from the sea. Rain was lashing down and there were patches of white water around Dolphin Rock. We decided to abandon filming for the day, and the crew set off for their base in Audierne. Even so, by wildlife filming standards, it was classified as an excellent day.

During the idyllic morning Peter Gillbe had telephoned James Wharram and told him to head for Brittany as conditions were perfect. At that time the lighthouse at Cape Finisterre had appeared quite close because its silhouette was clearly visible. Now, half-lost in the grey mist, it appeared to be a long way off, and through my binoculars I could see the water pounding up around the base, and spray being flung high into the air.

In the morning the canoe men had said they were disappointed because there was no surf. That afternoon I could see them through my binoculars riding giant rollers that pounded up the beach which earlier had been covered with holiday-makers basking in the sun. The heads of the waves were blown into a fine spume before they eventually collapsed, transformed into seething white foam that washed up the totally empty beach. It was awesome and spectacular, and I could well understand why the Baie des Trépassés was sometimes translated into English as the Bay of Tragedy. Any yacht moored in the bay that lost its moorings would quickly have become a wreck on the shore.

I went back to my room having decided that I would not be the last person Jean Louis would see that day. During the evening, as I stood luxuriating beneath a hot shower, I wondered what the dolphin was doing now that her human friends had deserted her. Was she swimming around the unattended boats which were bobbing like corks and snatching at their moorings in the little bay beside Dolphin Rock? Listening to the storm rattling the shutters, I also wondered if James Wharram had set sail from Cornwall with his young and mainly inexperienced crew.

Early the next morning Peter Scoones, Georgie Douwma and I, all clutching underwater cameras and dressed in wetsuits, jumped into the sea that surged round the steps in the tiny harbour. The water was like grey soup. We swam out to the Humber inflatable on its mooring and then set off to see if we could find Jean Louis. Although the wind had abated somewhat there still was a very heavy swell, and it was extremely uncomfortable aboard the inflatable. We went for a very bumpy ride well beyond Dolphin Rock and I had to hold tight to avoid being bounced out when we travelled fast enough to remain on the plane. When Jean Louis did not honour us with her presence we aborted our mission, adjourning to the hotel where, still dressed in our wetsuits, we joined the other guests and were served breakfast. The hot coffee and fresh bread were dispatched with that French early-morning phlegm which is indicative of a race who would prefer to avoid mornings altogether and start the day at lunchtime.

During breakfast Peter Gillbe telephoned England and learned that James Wharram had not left but proposed to sail that evening, if the weather forecast remained favourable.

However, for a day that had started so unpromisingly, Tuesday turned out to be special in several ways. We returned to the harbour after breakfast, and just as I slid into the water Jean Louis appeared out of the haze with a clear plastic bag on the tip of her beak. At first I thought it odd that she should have swum into the bag and did not know how to dislodge it, but that thought was quickly dismissed. When she got close to me she let the plastic go, and then, as the bag drifted gently through the water, swept round in a circle and caught it on her pectoral fin. Continuing her fly past, she disappeared at high speed as if she were a magician saying 'Now you see it, now you don't.' She reappeared seconds later with the plastic still on her fin, then let it go again, just in front of me. I put my hand up to take it and she swam past at high speed, whisking the plastic away from me. I was delighted. Jean Louis had initiated a game of her own accord. Unfortunately she had chosen to present me with the plastic bag just as the film camera had been handed back into the boat for reloading, and by the time it was back in the water the game was over and Jean Louis had disappeared. So we took a break and went back to sea later.

When we did so the sea was still very rough round Dolphin Rock but the water was clear. How I came to venture into that rough water is still surprising to me, and I will reveal what happened in the next chapter. However, on a return trip to film Jean Louis in the rough but clear water an uncommon fish called a John Dory swam past me and I chased after it through the kelp. As I did so a dark shadow passed over the scene. I looked up – and couldn't believe my eyes. A shark nearly twice the size of Jean Louis was passing overhead. At first glance I thought it was a huge hammerhead, but when I took a second look I realised it did not have the unmistakeable head of what is reputed to be one of the most dangerous sharks in the sea. It was a giant basking shark. I swam as fast as my flailing fins would propel me towards Peter Scoones, the underwater camera-man. Both of us had filmed before in tropical seas, so I made a sign with my hand which I knew he would understand meant 'shark'. At first Peter looked at me as if I were suffering from the hallucinations of nitrogen narcosis. Then, when I pointed over his shoulder with all the urgent emphasis I could muster, he looked up. As soon as he registered two shapes swimming over him, one much larger than the other, he brought his viewfinder up to his eye. He managed to get just a short sequence of Jean Louis escorting the shark firmly out of her territory as they swam side by side out of visibility.

When we were discussing the incident later, Peter looked

at me and with a twinkle in his eye said, 'Horace, I really thought you'd gone off your rocker when you rushed up to me doing the shark signal.' As an afterthought – and Peter is not given to using superlatives, even in the most mind-boggling circumstances – he added, 'He was quite impressive, wasn't he?'

Although we had filmed Jean Louis with a shark, from a scientific point of view the more significant of the two events was the fact that the dolphin had initiated a new game. This was something I could develop and report to the scientific community. So the next day I went into the water with a planned experiment, and I made sure that Peter had a full magazine of film in his Arriflex before I started. In the pocket of my lifejacket I had a variety of shapes and colours of pieces of plastic. My plan was to develop the game and then to present pieces of plastic to the dolphin one by one, to find out which colour and shape she preferred. However, Jean Louis had different plans and took absolutely no notice of my offerings, no matter how tantalisingly I presented them to her. Then, quite by chance, I picked up the folding anchor of the inflatable. This caught her attention immediately, so I hastily stuffed all the pieces of plastic back into the pouch of my lifejacket and had her undivided attention for five minutes while I manipulated the anchor in a way to produce the maximum noise – which I could hear even through the thick neoprene of my wetsuit hood.

I wondered whether it was the anchor itself that interested her, or the noise it made. When I later showed her several different anchors Jean Louis showed no special interest in any of them, thereby quashing any experiments I might have developed to establish what it was about anchors that had stimulated her in the first place.

However, even though I had failed to conduct experiments to follow through my observations on the dolphin's one-off obsessions with anchors and plastic bags, I did eventually succeed in getting a catamaran into La Baie des Trépassés – or at least, James Wharram did.

James arrived two days after we had started filming, and

Jean Louis escorted the *Teheni* into the bay. Even before the catamaran was securely anchored, Carola, unable to wait any longer to make contact with the dolphin, leapt, with a shriek of delight and completely naked, into the sea.

· 6 ·

A Closer Encounter

The arrival of our floating base enabled me to start work on the experiment I was most keen to conduct. This was based on the fact that dolphins are members of the whale family and are therefore air-breathing mammals. When dolphins surface to breathe, the complete inhalation and exhalation cycle takes place in a very short time, usually less than a second, and is accompanied by a sharp puff. The large baleen whales give away their presence on the surface by their characteristic 'blows', which are very vigorous and send fountains of spray into the air. Humpback whales also expel air under-water, when engaged in a remarkable method of fishing called 'bubble netting'. This entails the whale swimming below the surface and emitting a fine stream of bubbles from the blow-hole. As it swims it describes a circle, or a figure-of-eight, around a shoal of fish. The thin screen of glistening bubbles, rising like a curtain through the water, alarms the fish, which concentrate in the centre of the net of bubbles. While the fish are temporarily trapped, the open-mouthed humpback rushes upwards through the tube of bubbles it has created, engulfing fish as it goes. The end of this advanced food-gathering procedure is usually signalled on the surface by a spectacular breach as the whale bursts through the surface of the sea swallowing its prey.

I knew that Jean Louis could also voluntarily exhale under-water as I had often seen her sending plumes of bubbles to the surface from her blow-hole. My experiment was based on persuading her to do this in a controlled manner and thereby raising a submerged object, such as a lobster pot, to the surface. If she would do that when I wanted her to, I could justly claim a cooperative bond between man and dolphin.

With the help of the crew of the *Teheni*, principally James's Dutch co-designer and navigator, Hanneke Boon, I constructed a large square frame from light pieces of timber. To one corner of this we attached a small bundle of lead weights, sufficiently heavy to hold the frame securely on the sea bed when it was submerged. My plan was to put the frame on the floor of the sea near the catamaran and let Jean Louis examine it. When she had grown accustomed to its presence I proposed to swim through the frame and encourage the dolphin to do likewise. The next part of the plan would be to attach a bucket to the top of the frame and feed into it sufficient air from my regulator to make it buoyant. The decisive stage would come when Jean Louis was accustomed to having the entire structure on the sea bed, and was happy to swim back and forth through it. I would then show her how she could lift it to the surface simply by blowing out through her blow-hole under the bucket.

An advantage of working with people who build boats is that the task of constructing pieces of experimental equipment can quickly be accomplished. In a very short time my experimental frame was lowered to the sea bed, watched by Jean Louis, who always came across to see what was going on when we attempted something new. She seemed to accept its presence in her world immediately, then became bored and swam away. I managed to call her back by clapping some stones together, and immediately showed her how to swim through the frame. But she showed only fleeting interest before disappearing from view.

The next time she came by I thought I would do something more interesting, and therefore more likely to maintain her attention. I attached the plastic bucket to the top of the frame and put a little air in it. This operation she certainly watched with more than a fleeting interest. When I had completed the task, I swam a short distance away to let the sediment I had stirred up settle. I remained suspended in the water, admiring my handiwork. As a piece of experimental equipment it worked beautifully. The lead weights held one corner of the eight-foot-square frame on the sand. Being wood, it tended to float and automatically assumed an upright position in the water. The plastic bucket, partly filled with air and attached to the uppermost corner, further helped to pull the frame into a vertical position. I swam into the centre of the frame, which was large enough to accommodate both myself and the dolphin. Positioning myself directly under the bucket, I took the mouthpiece out of my mouth and exhaled. The bubbles rose into the bucket and gave sufficient extra buoyancy for the entire assembly to rise smoothly to the surface as I swam out of the frame. I looked around, expecting to get at least an interested nod from Jean Louis, but was disappointed to find she had lost all interest in the business and was nowhere to be seen.

I cannot pretend I was not irritated by her lack of interest. I looked at Peter Scoones, who was there to record my breakthrough, but all he did was shrug his shoulders and wait for me to bring my confounded contraption back down to the sea bed again. This I did simply by swimming to the surface and emptying the air from the bucket. Hanneke and one of her assistants looked anxiously over the side of the *Teheni* to see how I was getting on. The rest of the crew were lounging, mostly naked, on the deck, sunbathing. 'It's all right for some,' I mumbled into my regulator as I swam back down to Peter, who was still waiting patiently for Jean Louis. She had clearly found some alternative trivial activity in the bay far more interesting than my profound research experiment. She did condescend to return when I again clapped two stones together, but swam away immediately when she saw I had nothing new to offer.

Well, if that experiment failed I would have to try something else. That is what science is all about, I told myself.

So I directed my thoughts along other lines, and set up a further experiment based upon primary but different characteristics of the two animals I was trying to bring together – namely that dolphins are acoustic and humans manipulative.

Humans could certainly not survive anywhere but in the tropical regions of the world if they were unable to produce tools and manipulate their surroundings. Even the tropical rain forests support only a relatively small human population, and those who inhabit these regions still depend for their survival to a large extent on the primitive hunting weapons they manufacture.

Dolphins need a high calorie intake to survive the cold and provide energy for their vigorous hunting activities. They use sonar to detect the fish they hunt, and it has also been suggested that they use directional sonar to stun their prey. Indeed, it is hard to imagine how dolphins would survive in conditions of low visibility if they could not 'see with sound'.

I had already come to the conclusion that while creating new visual images was not a reliable means of attracting and maintaining Jean Louis' attention, she always responded if I generated a sound, and would devote more than passing attention to a new one. To test this observation, I needed to create an experimental situation which would generate sound. If I could get the dolphin to manipulate something that created sound, then I could claim to have started her thinking in more mechanical human terms.

I felt quite smug about the solution I came up with, and was hopeful that Jean Louis would find quite irresistible the underwater xylophone I would build for her.

We found a rusty old anchor on the seabed, which would provide the weighted frame I needed for my new musical instrument. Next I needed some sound generators. These were available in considerable quantities aboard the *Teheni*, as by-products of our effort to drain the French wine lake. Hanneke helped me attach, with lengths of nylon string about 18 inches long, six empty wine bottles to the heavy shank of the anchor. A small pear-shaped Perrier water bottle was attached by a length of cord to the metal bar, to act as the hammer. The underwater xylophone, which we called a Dobbsophone, was then lowered over the side on to the sandy sea bed beneath the *Teheni*. I swam down, untangled the lines, filled the bottles with air from my regulator and proudly admired my handiwork. All the bottles bobbed upright like submerged corks at the ends of the lines that were tied to the anchor. I took hold of the Perrier bottle and tapped the wine bottles in turn. They made very clear, audible sounds, all of roughly the same note. Then I tuned each of the bottles to make a different note by letting out some of the air. An underwater microphone, connected to a recorder on board, was lowered over the side of the *Teheni*. Peter had rigged synchronised sound to his camera, and Duncan Gibbons, a film director who was paying us a visit, acted as clapper-boy, tapping the clapper-board with a spanner to make a better sound. The cameras were rolling as I played my first underwater concerto on my homemade xylophone. As I hammered away with gusto, I thought the results impressive. So too did Jean Louis, who had watched the setting up of the underwater recording film studio with her usual curiosity. However, such was my involvement with creating underwater music that I did not notice her swim away after I had played the first few notes.

When Jean Louis failed to reappear I surfaced and asked for the folding anchor from the inflatable. Jean Louis came back when it was lowered down to me complete with a length of chain. Having regained her attention, I tried to direct Jean Louis towards the Dobbsophone and showed her slowly but very clearly that by gently pushing the Perrier bottle she could create a sound. Despite several attempts to persuade her to do so, she showed no inclination whatever to make the sound for herself. Indeed, she showed more interest in the anchor and became fascinated whenever I moved it. Listening to the tapes later, we discovered that the anchor and its chain made many high-frequency sounds, most of which were inaudible to the human ear.

Another experiment which produced a disappointing result at the time, but later revealed an interesting facet of how dolphins perceive their environment, concerned the use of a mirror. With Donald, I had set out deliberately to confuse the dolphin by showing him his image in a mirror. I knew the reflected image he saw with his eyes would not correspond with his sonar image, which would indicate the rectangular shape of the sheet of glass. His response was immediate. He attacked it and smashed it to smitherines by ramming it with his beak, destroying the mirror in the same way he might have killed a threatening shark. I concluded that seeing his image really had confused Donald, and that he destroyed the mirror to protect me from a possible, though unidentifiable, source of danger. An alternative, although I think less likely, explanation advanced by a fellow scientist was that he did not like seeing another dolphin in his territory, and tried to dispose of the intruder.

To avoid the repetition of the hazards from broken glass, I took a large plastic mirror down to confuse Jean Louis. Unlike Donald, she showed no signs of confusion. She took an interested look at her reflection and then swam away. At the time we filmed this experiment we were running synchronised sound with the film. It was not until months later, when we were in the editing studio, that we found an acceptable explanation for Jean Louis' unresponsive behaviour. Prior to her coming into view, we could hear dolphin sounds which indicated that long before I could see her she was examining me, and the mirror I was carrying, with her sonar. However, as soon as she swam into vision she switched off her sonar, obviously using her eyes instead. Like a pilot coming into a foggy airfield she had used her sonar like radar, to navigate and give a general view, before changing to vision for a more highly defined image of nearby objects. Her lack of response to seeing her reflection I attributed to the fact that she was a female, quite different in personality to Donald, who at times was assertively masculine.

Donald had demonstrated his assertiveness very clearly when I used an aquaplane, which is a board with handles. As I was being pulled through the water, the dolphin nipped one of my elbows progressively harder with his front teeth until I was compelled to let go, whereupon he took the board in his mouth and attempted to gain a free ride, just as I had done. He was not successful, for the board was made of rigid plastic and kept slipping out of his mouth when his teeth failed to grip it. I was very aware of the effectiveness of his teeth, for when I removed my wetsuit I discovered Donald had bitten right through it leaving a row of bleeding punctures on my elbow. What I found particularly interesting about that incident was the way in which the dolphin progressively dominated the situation. At first he just butted me gently with his head to inform me that he wanted to play with the aquaplane. I knew exactly what he wanted, but I refused to let it go from my hands. It then became a tustle for supremacy with the dolphin becoming more vigorous in his efforts to dislodge me. I was fully aware that the 700-pound dolphin could annihilate me in an instant by ramming me with his beak. So when he really started to assert himself by biting me I conceded to his wishes.

Jean Louis obviously loved it when I rode the same aquaplane through her territory. She would accompany me, sometimes keeping closely alongside, but more often staying just behind my trailing fins. As befitted her gentle disposition, she never attempted to dislodge me from the aquaplane.

One of the problems of filming such an event underwater in limited visibility is that the aquaplane is in view to the cameraman only for the relatively short time it takes to pass by. Peter Gillbe said that he would like a more sustained head-on shot, a close-up of me holding the handle and being pulled through the water at speed. It is exhilarating being yanked head-first through the water while holding on like grim death to the handles of the aquaplane.

Being towed backwards is an even wilder experience, as Peter Scoones found out when he volunteered to attempt to get the shot, which he decided could be achieved if he was attached to a second rope and pulled along backwards, just ahead of me. So, with some misgivings, Georgie tied the end of a stout rope round Peter's ankles and watched him sink rapidly beneath the boat. Peter had put on plenty of extra weight so that he wouldn't rise to the surface while being towed along. Holding on to the aquaplane, I quickly followed. Georgie put the engine into gear and reluctantly moved off. She felt a snatch when the ropes went taut but had no communication with us once we were submerged. I felt the pull on my arms and the pressure building up on my mask as the water started rushing past my head.

By directing the leading edge of the board I could control my depth and move from side to side. Peter, however, clinging desperately to his camera, was quite unable to prevent himself from rotating like a fishing spinner. If he had shot the sequence I would have looked like a spinning underwater kamikaze pilot on a mission – which was exactly how Peter looked to me. I surfaced quickly and hauled up the dizzy cameraman. He grinned and said he would try another approach. After several more attempts we eventually achieved the desired result by tying one of Peter's legs to the aquaplane rope. In this way I had some control as we were towed in tandem, head to head, through the water. What Jean Louis made of this whole bizarre episode I have no idea. I suspect she found it entertainingly idiotic, like a lot of other human activities.

One of the tenets of scientific investigation is that rigid conclusions should not be drawn from single experiments that cannot be repeated by other investigators. Jean Louis was certainly demonstrating the dangers of generalisation, and of expecting all dolphins to comply with an often romanticised norm. When studying behaviour, one should be aware that the differences between one dolphin and another may be as great as those between one person and another. This had become dramatically apparent to me during the spell of very rough weather immediately before the *Teheni*'s arrival.

The water around Dolphin Rock was a ragged mass of turbulent white foam. We went as close as we dared in the inflatable to investigate what had looked like a seal floating close to the rocks. When we got close we saw that it was Jean Louis, floating upright in the water like a fishing float, with about a third of her body above water. We approached quietly. The dolphin's eyes were shut and she quivered. For one moment I thought she was in the throes of death, because she was in spasm and obviously unaware of our presence. Then she opened her eyes and, as if suddenly awakened from sleep, dived beneath the sea to reappear behaving normally alongside the inflatable a few moments later. Having first-hand knowledge of the behaviour of many large animals under the influence of morphine-like drugs, I am convinced that we caught her unexpectedly in a self-induced trance-spasm initiated by the wild water. When I put on my fins, mask and snorkel she led me closer and closer to the rocks. I peered down. Through the swirling clouds of suspended bubbles I got a glimpse of the dolphin riding the undersea currents like a roller-coaster. She was inviting me down. I swam away from the rocks, climbed back into the inflatable, put on my aqualung and followed her siren call. She led me into the most exhilarating dive I had ever had in my twenty-five years' diving career.

The sea was like a giant jacuzzi in which I was twirled and swirled by foaming currents as they rushed between the rocks. The kelp flailed like palm trees in a hurricane. However, with Jean Louis always near me, I experienced no sense of fear, only an increasing feeling of intense excitement. When I was very close to a rock-face it appeared to flash past. Then it stopped and accelerated away at enormous speed in another direction. It was an illusion, of course, similar to that experienced when sitting in a stationary train and watching an adjacent train move away. In my case, it had the opposite effect, for it was the rocks that were stationary, while I was suspended in the sea, being rushed back and forth in the current.

I realised that I was safe provided I stayed well beneath the surface. Under-water, the sea does not bump against rocks but sweeps past them. My thick wetsuit and neoprene gloves protected me from abrasions. Swimming with Jean Louis in the underwater turmoil, I could see that it was in conditions like these that she had acquired some of the many scars and superficial marks on her body.

The danger zone is the interface between air, rock and water. If I was thrown on the rocks, or tried to climb out, I would quickly have been battered to death because of the weight of my body. Under-water I was virtually weightless and moved like thistledown blown by the wind. The inflatable was also safe provided it kept away from the rocks, and when I decided to return to the above-water world of humans, I swam well clear of Dolphin Rock before surfacing and giving the hand signal that I wanted to be picked up. Georgie manoeuvred the Humber alongside me in seconds. As soon as I climbed aboard I poured out my feelings in a torrent of words. I had never felt so elated in my life before.

What I did not know at that moment was that while I had been down, intoxicated by the power of the undersea storm and my new-found ability to survive in it, a life and death struggle had been taking place near by. Two anglers fishing from the shore had been swept by a freak wave into the ocean. One of them, whose severe injuries included several broken bones, was pulled from the water by a helicopter rescue team. The other was drowned, his body lost.

I went into the rough sea around Dolphin Rock again the next day to re-enact my experiences for the benefit of our underwater cameraman. We little knew as we filmed that the unrecovered body of the drowned angler was being swept by the current past Dolphin Rock. When we broke for lunch, a helicopter appeared and raised the corpse from an isolated beach a short distance from where we had been diving. The Bay of Lost Souls, or Bay of Tragedies, had claimed yet another victim.

The ancient myth that dolphins will always go to the aid of a drowning man was also tested and found wanting. I have no doubt that in the past dolphins have sometimes helped drowning humans, but the incident with Jean Louis showed quite clearly that deliverance by dolphins cannot be guaranteed.

Jean Louis seemed to be turning life on its side and causing all of us to look at it from new angles. Peter Gillbe soon appreciated that, as the director of the film, he had no control whatsoever over its star. As time went by and our pre-conceived plans were either not fulfilled, or worked out in a manner completely different to our expectations, Peter accepted the situation. With a wry smile, he would say, 'Horace, go in the water and see what Jean Louis wants to do today.' What we did next depended almost entirely on what Jean Louis decided we should do.

She became bored with my experiments fairly quickly, but she never tired of playing games, especially when the sea was rough. As the days passed, we spent more and more time simply playing together. Jean Louis made me shed any inhibitions I might have had as a middle-aged man soon to become a grandfather. Under the sea with her, the experiments lost their importance and I didn't even have the responsibility of having to shoot film – that was Peter's job. I became a child again. At first we just played tag, racing after one another through the kelp-fringed gulleys around Dolphin Rock. Then the games became progressively more complex. Hide-and-seek was one of my favourites. I would rush away from Jean Louis and sink into the kelp, holding my breath for as long as I could. Sometimes she found me, sometimes she didn't before I could hold my breath no longer and the exhaust bubbles from my aqualung gave my hideout away. One of her favourite tricks was to swim just a few inches behind my fins, where the restricted vision of my facemask prevented me from seeing her. I would swim through the seascape and peer behind rocks unaware that she was closely trailing me. Once I discovered she liked doing this, I would suddenly turn round, as if we were playing 'What's the time, Mr Wolf?' When I reacted and yelled 'Dinner time!' into my mouthpiece, she would fin rapidly away, with me in hot pursuit. Then, as I turned a corner she would meet me face to face before hurtling off again towards the cameraman, who was desperately trying to keep up with both of us and film at the same time.

By the end of our stay I had long since come to realise that Jean Louis was the senior member of our partnership. When I had shed sufficient of my human arrogance to accept the possibility that she was teaching me, rather than doing what I wanted her to, I could see how subtle she had been. Right at the beginning she had demonstrated how to play with a piece of plastic, but as soon as I started to get serious, she just quietly refused to cooperate. Peter Gillbe was probably more aware of this as a bystander, and accepted it, despite his resolution to make a film along the lines we originally planned. Peter spent much of his time in the serious business of making party-political films. Jean Louis caused even him to change his attitudes. His sense of humour came to the fore when deciding the credits for the film. Next to his name, in bold letters on the running captions, came the title ASSISTANT DIRECTOR – JEAN LOUIS.

The film was eventually shown on Christmas Day, 1985 at 1.30 p.m. on Channel 4, and watched by 900,000 people throughout Britain. For me it was a fine prelude to a traditional lunch enjoyed with my family – including my beautiful 10-month-old granddaughter Rebecca, who was born after we had finished filming.

The film was entitled by Peter *A Closer Encounter*, with no apologies to a film with a similar name which portrayed the arrival on earth of an alien intelligence.

In my studies with Jean Louis I had made virtually no progress towards harnessing dolphin intelligence to help mankind exploit the riches of the sea. But Jean Louis had pulled back the curtains just sufficiently to suggest that dolphins had something very special to offer us – even if it wasn't a partnership in the use of the sea's resources with man taking the dominant role.

· 7 ·

A Robinson Crusoe Day

Everyone involved with the filming project was affected by it, but for some it was a much more profound experience than for others. It reflected the personality of the individual concerned, and his or her needs. One person for whom meeting Jean Louis was extremely significant was Carola Hepp – a tall, statuesque German who combined hard-working practical abilities with extensive artistic talents that included painting, composing and playing songs, as well as writing prose and poetry in German and English. One of the few items she took aboard the *Teheni* was her guitar, and by the time the catamaran had reached France Carola had composed a song about the boat and the joys of sailing on her. Carola also composed a beautiful song about dolphins, and late one dark night she sang it to a small group of us, sitting on the deck. We knew that Jean Louis was near, as we occasionally heard the characteristic puff of her breathing mixed with the night sounds of water lapping the hulls of the gently rocking catamaran. As Carola finished her song I saw in the lamplight a ghostly white figure rear out of the water, arch in a curve, and drop back into the sea with a splash that sent spray flying over the musician and her audience. It was Jean Louis, and her leap left an image in my memory of a white dolphin, suspended in mid-air, and set in a pitch-black sky.

Carola had many images in her imagination and her dreams of dolphins, often spiralling towards infinity at the end of a tunnel. Carola was a sensitive and sensual person for whom it was important that she should be naked when in the water with Jean Louis – not 'a wrapped and tied-up parcel', as she described me in my wetsuit. We both noted how, in addition to her obvious excitement in rough water, Jean Louis enjoyed very gentle strokes on her body. One of the dolphin's favourite pastimes was gliding up and down the anchor rope of the catamaran in such a way that the rope rubbed her body from nose to tail. When she did this her eyes were often half-closed as if she was in a state of bliss.

Carola did not sail back to England on the *Teheni*. She left very early one morning to catch a train, and I ferried her ashore in the Humber inflatable. As we skimmed across the dark water Jean Louis, bathed in green pearls of phosphorescence, rushed through the sea maintaining station just ahead of our bows. It was a fitting farewell gesture.

In an article entitled 'Daze with a Dolphin' Carola wrote:

> Looking back to the few days living on the catamaran, I see a sentence that is not finished, an astonishment never revealed, and the inability on my side to understand, to understand more.

At the end of the article she commented on the spontaneous nature of the dolphin's responses to the setting-up of my experiments, and suggested that Jean Louis got bored when nothing exciting in her terms happened afterwards. She also called into question the significance of doing experiments:

> Is the scientific approach perhaps something that does not fit her? Science is so tight leaving few possibilities. Life is not only 'Yes' and 'No'. There is truth in-between that we sometimes know, but more often than not refuse to see, or still cannot see, because there is nothing to prove it.
>
> So the possibilities of science might be too limited, too narrow-minded for a creature that perhaps has a different kind of intelligence.

8 *Above left*: Percy and the author off Godrevy Island.
9 *Above right*: Judy was delighted with this snapshot she took of Percy.
10 Percy was intrigued but not impressed when Bob played my underwater xylophone made from wine bottles and an old anchor.

11 Filming Percy as he rides the bow wave of the *Tar dor Moor* on an idyllic summer's evening.

12-13 Both Percy (*below left*) and Jean Louis (*below right*) were fascinated by anchors and anchor chains.

Having accounted for the failure of my experiments, Carola concluded her article with a suggestion that sprang from her own deep and much explored feelings towards dolphins.

Watching her and reminiscing how I feel, she was so sensitive and so sensual that we should have played more with her, not with devices – spontaneously with our bodies and all our sensuality and art, with music and dances full of joy, so that she perhaps could have had a chance to show us her dance, her games, her body, to teach us what she knows – because who is more intelligent than a creature who wants to teach?

Carola knew what I was doing with my experiments when I worked on the surface. However, I spent much of my time under-water, completely hidden from Carola's view, and she did not see the games the dolphin and I played together. Even so, the ideas she expressed in print were closely aligned to the conclusions I had come to. By the time I left Brittany I had decided to continue my scientific approach, but at the same time to try to respond much more spontaneously in any future contacts with wild dolphins.

The opportunity for pursuing both these lines of investigation was waiting for me in Cornwall when I returned on the overnight ferry to Plymouth from St Malo on 7 August, 1983, for during my absence in France contact had been maintained with Percy, the wild dolphin in Portreath.

It is hard to imagine a greater contrast in life-style than for a schoolgirl, who lives in the heart of England, to go to sea aboard a Polynesian catamaran with a group as unconventional as those aboard the *Teheni*. Yet that is what Sarah, the daughter of Tricia Kirkman, did when she was fifteen years old. She shared a berth with Carola, in the close confines of one of the hulls of the *Teheni*, on which she was the youngest member of the crew. Sarah, who was seldom short of a pithy, and often humorous, retort when questioned about her experiences, was self-assured and fast becoming a vivacious young lady. Even so, her mother was anxious about her well-being and travelled to Cornwall to await the return of her daughter. Judy Holborn kindly provided Tricia with a bed in the office at Beach House.

All the residents were fast asleep when I arrived at Beach House, direct from Plymouth, in the early hours. The sea was covered with white horses and over breakfast Bob said it was too rough to take his inflatable to sea in search of Percy. Ruth Wharram had stayed behind to look after the base in Devoran while her husband, James, was in France. As I could not go out to see Percy, and knowing that Ruth was anxious to discover how we had fared with Jean Louis, I motored across the heel of Cornwall to have lunch with her and tell her the news.

I could afford to spend only one more full day in Cornwall, and I was anxious to make contact with Percy again before journeying to London. I thought my wish had been granted when the wind dropped during the evening and I was lulled to sleep by the gentle swish of the sea and the occasional squawk of the gulls carried through the open window on the hot, still night air.

Tricia Kirkman's interest in dolphins was aroused when I showed the film during my first visit to Beach House, but she was far too reticent to ask Bob to take her out to see Percy because she could not swim and had never been to sea. Her desire to see Percy overcame her fear when she learned how her daughter Sarah had coped with sailing across the English Channel on the *Teheni* to see Jean Louis in France. Bob needed only the slightest excuse to take a real dolphin enthusiast out to see Percy, and said that if we put Tricia in a wetsuit, which would act as a lifejacket, she would be just as safe – well, nearly as safe – as the two of us. He did admit, however, that she would have to be prepared for a bumpy ride, as the wind had risen.

People who have not been to sea often have little idea what conditions are like when they sit on the shore on a breezy summer's day and see white caps on the tops of the blue waves. As we sat having breakfast at a table on the lawn outside Beach House, I knew full well that we would be in for a very uncomfortable ride. But I saw no point in drawing this to Tricia's attention. I was anxious to get going, because I could see by looking at the waves crashing on the beach that they were approaching the stage where it would not be possible to launch the inflatable. So we encased Tricia in an ancient black wetsuit and humped the inflatable down the beach, pushing off when a couple of smaller than usual waves broke. Even so the bows of the Zodiac reared like a bucking bronco, but we managed to keep her head to sea. Thankfully the motor started at the first pull and we were able to move away from the danger zone close to shore. The sea between Gull Rock and the nearby headland was very rough. One minute we were down in a trough with mountains of sea all around us. The next we were perched on the top of a wave and rushing like a toboggan into the next trough. Bob was an experienced and superb boat-handler. He knew just when to throttle back and steer the inflatable so that we would not take too much water over the side.

Inflatable boats are designed to travel on the plane. To do that they must go relatively fast. The faster you go the harder you hit the waves and the more spray comes flying aboard. Poor Tricia must have been terrified as she sat on one of the tubes of the inflatable clinging tightly to the hand ropes. It wasn't until we returned that I noticed her knuckles bleeding where the skin had been rubbed off by the constant battering. However, she kept her fears to herself and even managed to smile at Bob when he asked her to move forward because her long hair, soaked by the spray and blown by the wind, started to lash his face. She had not realised that as we bumped over successive waves she was being vibrated towards the stern of the boat.

Eventually we reached Godrevy Island, where Bob hoped we would meet up with Percy. Sure enough we did find the dolphin, busy inspecting the lobster pots cast overboard from a small fishing vessel called *Joker*. We arrived just as they had finished laying a string of pots and Bob was anxious that Percy should stay with us and not go with the fishing boat as it headed north towards the Stones, which Bob knew was one of the dolphin's favourite haunts.

Tricia's fears vanished completely when Percy swam alongside, and she was even more delighted when he came up to inspect a wooden paddle Bob put in the water to attract the dolphin's attention while I kitted up in my aqualung.

In a short time I rolled backwards into the water and said hello to Percy's cheeky face as it came into vision out of the gloom. With an underwater visibility of less than twelve feet I could not see his tail when he hovered head-on to me. I stayed under the boat and got a dolphin's-eye view of the paddle Bob had immersed in the water. I was pleased that Percy would allow such physical contact, which was more than had been achieved with Jean Louis despite her six years of association with humans. The dolphin also allowed Bob to touch him briefly from the boat with his hands. We were anchored very close to the rocks. I swam over the dark kelp forest between the island and the shore until I saw the kelp fronds bending over in one direction and knew that I was getting into the current. Percy followed me for some way and then returned to the counter-attraction of Bob waving the paddle in the water. When I returned to the inflatable I clung to the side and asked Bob to pull up his anchor, which was similar in design to the folding anchor Jean Louis had found so fascinating. Bob complied with my request, and when the anchor, which was on the end of a chain, was in mid-water he jigged it up and down. Percy, hovering under the boat, also watched it with intense interest for a few seconds. Then he whooshed away like a rocket out of a milk bottle.

Despite many hours at sea Bob quickly became seasick with the motion of a stationary boat, especially when he was restricted inside a tight wetsuit. I saw the pallor of his face when he pulled up the anchor, and knew immediately that he was suffering from *mal de mer*, so I quickly climbed aboard. We rowed the boat ashore on the smooth sand of Godrevy Beach where the sea was not rough because it was in the lee of the island, and Bob recovered quickly when he felt firm ground beneath his feet. We sat on the beach drinking the coffee Judy had provided, surrounded by holiday-makers, most of whom were unaware of the dolphin fishing in the current between the shore and the nearby island. His presence was detected only by those with sharp eyes who happened to notice a dorsal fin rise swiftly and silently for a second as the dolphin rose to take a breath before descending again into the turbulent water.

When Bob had recovered we easily launched the inflatable into the gentle waves. Percy joined us a short distance off-shore and Tricia had the thrill of watching him race alongside as we turned in circles and did figures-of-eight in the channel between the island and the headland. Even so I noted that Percy would not be enticed away from the zone I had identified as his territory for the day. Having watched Jean Louis follow a zig-zagging inflatable from under-water I knew how well she could manoeuvre. But Bob was very reluctant to go too fast and turn too quickly for fear of clipping the dolphin with his whizzing propeller, thus slicing, with the ease of a circular saw, into any piece of Percy's body that came into contact with it.

Even though we were moving, and he was handling the boat with his usual skill, Bob started to feel seasick again. We decided to land on Godrevy Island. It was low water on a big spring tide and many rocks that would normally be covered were exposed. We cruised into a gulley, the sides of which would be submerged under fifteen feet or more of water when the tide rose in about six hours' time. The glistening rocks were covered in mussels. We pulled off the largest ones as if we were selectively picking succulent blackberries and soon had a large bag full. We were all children again on our own Robinson Crusoe island.

Arriving at the landing stage for the island, we scaled some bronze rungs fixed to the rocks. The lighthouse had once been manned and evidence of its former occupants became apparent as we climbed towards the deserted buildings on top of the island. There was a walled garden, overgrown with weeds, and outside the derelict house an old water-tank turned on its side provided a shanty home for a family of young cormorants who noisily huddled in the back when we discovered their refuge.

From the top of the island, the Stones, more exposed than usual because of the exceptionally low tide, stretched north like a row of giant, malevolent black teeth. On the lee of the island the sea slid gently up and down the rocks, but on the windward side it surged over them creating short-lived blankets of boiling white foam. From our high vantage point we could see every detail of the beautiful Cornish seascape stretching to St Ives in one direction and to St Agnes Head in the other. Directly beneath us the ruffled water between the island and the shore was stained brown by the effluent from the river. As the tide started to rise the current through the straits became progressively stronger and the sea more turbulent.

When we eventually descended to the inflatable Bob assured Tricia that the ride back to Portreath would be slightly less bumpy as we would be going with the wind instead of into it. We cast off and had to run the gauntlet through the tortured, ragged water squeezed through the straits before getting into the larger, more regular swell of the open sea, where we had a wonderful time surfing along with a following wind.

About half-way to Portreath Bob suddenly slowed down and we spun round to inspect a dark object floating on the water. It was a sunfish, nearly two feet across. I say across, because the sunfish is most unusual: its body is very roughly disc-shaped, and unlike most other flat fish found in British waters, it does not feed on the bottom and therefore does not have both eyes on one side of its body like a plaice. It is dark grey in colour, and although it swims vertically in the water it is called a sunfish because of its habit of floating horizontally, like a saucer, apparently sunbathing. In this position its large dorsal and ventral fins, which project from the rim of the disc, look like wings. When disturbed it quickly turns upright and swims away. Bob told me at a later date that he once spotted a sunfish when Percy was swimming alongside his inflatable. He stopped and slowly circled the fish, as he had done with us, to give his full load of passengers a close look at the bizarre fish. They were most disappointed when it dived out of sight, but not for long, because Percy nosed it to the surface, and when it managed to escape by wriggling he promptly dived again and brought it back for another public appearance.

We didn't have the benefit of Percy's company when we encountered the sunfish on our return from Godrevy Island, and were therefore denied the opportunity of seeing it for a second time. We did, however, pay a visit to Ralph's Cupboard, and I enjoyed again the feeling of awe and wonder at being so close to those towering majestic cliffs.

At the base of the cliffs we found a seagull struggling in the water. It appeared to be uninjured but was very weak. As Tricia stroked the bird gently with her long fingers it calmed down. Bob said it probably had enteritis and that he would take it to the local seagull sanctuary. As we set off again the delicate bird recovered sufficient strength to snap at Tricia's hair as it fluttered in the wind.

Our Robinson Crusoe day ended on the grassy bank outside Beach House, where Bob and Judy prepared the mussels for their guests to eat for supper, washed down with the wine I had brought back from France. By the time we ate our al fresco meal the wind had died completely and the still air was as soft and warm as a duvet. The other guests wanted to know all about Percy, and in the notes I scribbled down just before I went to sleep I recorded a comment Bob made. 'Next year we'll be able to ride him.'

In the light of my experience with Jean Louis, who would not allow herself to be touched after six years, I felt we had a long way to go before we got to the stage where Percy would trust us sufficiently to allow us to touch and hold him, let alone for him to give us a ride. But the knowledge that Donald, another wild dolphin, had indeed towed both Bob and myself did give grounds for optimism.

I was still mulling over the subject when I set off early the next day, for I had agreed to return home via London where I planned to meet Peter Gillbe and unload some heavy equipment we had hired. I watched the sun rise over the harbour at Portreath, a deep orange disc in a blue-grey, mist-veiled sky which cleared as the warm air became scented with the smell of dry grass and ripening wheat. As the tarmac raced beneath my spinning wheels I thought of Bob, his boat loaded with excited guests, skimming across the water towards Godrevy Island. In my imagination I could hear the shrieks of delight when Percy was first sighted and sliced through the water towards the inflatable. It was hard to tear myself away.

My mind also switched to the other side of Cornwall and thoughts of the *Teheni* returning home. She had been delayed by the rough weather and I had no idea when she would make the final leg of her journey back to Devoran. I would dearly have liked to be there to welcome her when she arrived.

Late the following day I heard that the catamaran had berthed safely at high water alongside the Dolphin Link Headquarters.

· 8 ·

Disaster Strikes

Ten days after my return home from Cornwall I had a phone-call from Judy Holborn who told me that Percy had become progressively more rumbustious and playful since my visit. Bob had acquired a new engine for his inflatable and had been to sea every day taking guests out to see Percy. Such were the demands for the spontaneous dolphin-shows that Bob would take his inflatable from Portreath to Godrevy Sands where his clients were waiting on-shore. Bob would then ferry a boat-load out to Godrevy Island, which was where Percy was most frequently to be found. The dolphin soon got to know the sound of Bob's new engine and that it would be bringing him an appreciative audience. He would swim round the boat and then leap when it changed course or turned in a circle. However, those aboard, including Bob himself, could never be sure just when or where Percy would jump next. Having given the visitors an opportunity to enjoy the company of the wild dolphin, Bob would take the group back to the beach, returning after a short rest with a fresh load. The holiday-makers would enjoy the thrill of a boat ride, but, more important, they experienced the delight of sometimes touching the wild dolphin when Percy came right up to the inflatable. It was becoming a regular occurrence. The news spread. Visitors to Cornwall began congregating on the headland opposite Godrevy Island to watch the free dolphin-shows through their binoculars.

Judy, bubbling with enthusiasm, was very good at relating such events. But what she told me about Bob's dolphin excursions for their guests was a build-up to the main reason for her call, which was to report an exciting new aspect of Percy's behaviour.

A few days before she telephoned a couple of photographers had turned up to take some pictures for a German magazine. Bob trailed an inflated tyre inner-tube behind the boat and this caused Percy to put on his most spectacular display ever. He dived beneath the inflated ring, came up and peered through it. He flicked it through the air and was obviously delighted with this new turn of events because after a spell of playing with the tube he would come and rear out of the water to look directly at the passengers in the inflatable. Judy said the photographer should have got some superb pictures.

This set me thinking. One of the most successful of our experiments, with both Donald and Jean Louis, had been the aquaplane in which I was towed behind the boat. Sitting on my desk when I received the call from Judy was a diving magazine in which there was an advertisement for a new aquaplane manufactured by a professional diver. How would Percy react if I was towed along behind the boat in place of the inner-tube, I wondered.

I telephoned Paul Derby, the designer and manufacturer of the Hydro-fin, as the new aquaplane was called. From what he said it sounded a great improvement on the primitive, home-made device I had used previously. I was convinced that the dolphin would find a diver towed along under-water much more stimulating than a rubber ring towed on the surface, and that the Hydro-fin would provide another major step forward in the rapid advance that was being made in Percy's relationship with humans.

There were just a few days in which I could fit a visit to Cornwall prior to taking my family on holiday in Ireland. Time was short. Paul Derby agreed to supply me with a Hydro-fin and I volunteered to call and collect it in Essex on my way to Cornwall. I drove towards London on Bank Holiday Monday, 29 August. It was one of those rare times when the weather was kind to the multitudes of British workers taking a statutory day off from their toils. On the journey south the late afternoon sun beaming through the windows of my car gently burned my arms. The Meteorological Office announced over the car radio that it was the fourth hottest summer of the century, with 1976 taking the lead. That was the year Donald had behaved so unpredictably when I was towed on an aquaplane in St Ives Bay – an incident which was still very clear in my memory.

When I was presented with the Hydro-fin by Paul Derby that evening I discovered it was constructed of bright yellow plastic. It was considerably larger than my aquaplane, and being hollow floated when left unattended, whereas mine sank. It seemed ideal for my purpose in every way.

The sea shimmered under a clear blue sky when I arrived in Portreath at 2 p.m. the next day. I was greeted by Judy who, excited as ever, was keen to tell me the very latest developments in the rapidly unfolding Percy saga. The most important was her own personal experience. On one of the days when Bob could not go to Godrevy, Percy had come to see him, announcing his arrival with an astounding show of leaps in front of Beach House. This display was much appreciated by Judy who, unlike Bob, could not take long spells away from Beach House because of the needs of her guests. The sea was flat calm and Bob quickly put his inflatable to sea and urged Judy to join him. Judy was a little nervous, as she could barely swim, but her apprehension quickly evaporated when the dolphin continued his aquabatics, which she snapped with her cheap pocket camera. She produced the results for my inspection, showing me a succession of pictures in which she got closer and closer to Percy. Then, with the flourish of a true showwoman, she presented her *pièce de résistance*. Her final picture showed Percy fully airborne, and because of the angle from which the picture was taken it looked as though the dolphin was giving Bob a kiss. However, my praise hardly matched the tongue-in-cheek words Judy used when describing her own achievements as a photographer.

My vivacious hostess next revealed that she had been keen for me to see her pictures before I cast my eyes over the batch of pin-sharp enlargements produced by what she jokingly described as 'the competition'. On the lawn, as yet unintroduced to me, was the professional who had taken the photographs of Percy for the German magazine. He had brought some of his absolutely superb results with him and had presented Bob with a portfolio of black and white prints. She then introduced me to the photographer – who was known to everyone as Animal.

Animal was a burly Liverpudlian with a tousled mass of ginger hair and a curly ginger beard. He was one of those individualists that Liverpool seems to breed and export, who had emigrated to Cornwall with absolutely no intention of returning to his native city. He was a man to whom things were always happening, and he used this to his advantage in his job. As a result, Animal was a photographer who sometimes found himself in the news. A few days before our meeting he made headlines in a local paper for being rescued by the beautiful model he was photographing when he suddenly sank up to his chest in quicksand. He said he liked the challenge of 'hard news' photography, and showed me one of his cameras which had been smashed by a convicted murderer who didn't want to have his picture taken. I realised he was the kind of man who would not easily be deflected from his task. He told me there had been a number of threats on his life. Few people knew his real name, and he was happy to keep it that way. He was a true professional and could not afford to become emotionally involved with the many subjects he had to cover.

Animal was a good name for the photographer, and I liked him, especially when I discovered that as with most apparently hard men there was a soft side to him. He told me that of all the exciting and dangerous assignments he had been given, his commission to photograph Percy had had the most profound effect upon him. I think this was because in Percy he could recognise a fellow loner with a maverick spirit. He told me that many of the stories he covered made national headlines and that he seldom talked about his work – because it was work. Then along came a seemingly easy assignment which he had undertaken with his usual professionalism. To get some underwater shots he had put on a wetsuit and got in the sea with Percy, who seemed to take a devilish delight in attempting to frighten the wits out of the intrepid photographer by swirling around him like a speed boat under full power. The dolphin's finishing frightener was leaping high over Animal and crashing into the sea just beside him. That was an experience the hard-bitten photographer couldn't get out of his mind. It was something he wanted to talk about. And that was why he was back in Portreath. He wanted to see Percy again for the sheer joy of it.

He was not the only professional newsman to be affected in this way. When I was at home, between visits to Portreath, I had been telephoned by Geoffrey Lakeman, a staff reporter for the *Daily Mirror*. He told me he had spent a magical hour in the water with Percy, and felt so moved by the experience that he had brought his family to Portreath for the Bank Holiday. His encounter with Percy was used as a photo-spread in the *Daily Mirror* on 19 August, 1983. In the final paragraph Geoffrey Lakeman reported: 'My teeth were chattering, my hands and feet were blue with cold, but I've rarely experienced such a warm feeling.' I knew that feeling well, and told Geoffrey so when Judy introduced me to him. I chatted to the reporter and the photographer while we waited for Bob Holborn to return home.

When Bob eventually arrived he was in a glum mood because he had just been told how much it was going to cost to repair the radiator of his Volvo car. It was an expense neither of them welcomed at a time when Bob had stretched his financial resources to buy a new engine for his boat. Bob also admitted another cause for the lack of his usual cheerfulness.

'I'm worried about Percy,' he said. 'I think he's been hurt.'

When I quizzed him about the change in Percy's behaviour, Bob said that for the last few days the dolphin had seemed wary of the boat and would not allow himself to be stroked or even touched. I have to admit that I came to regard all the dolphins I have known in human terms, often thinking of them as people. 'I expect he's just been having an "off period",' I commented. Secretly confident that I could reverse the dolphin's depression by presenting Percy with an exciting new source of interest, I proudly showed Bob the Hydro-fin. Bob suggested we should go to sea as soon as possible, as we were approaching slack water and that was Percy's favourite time to play.

Bob's Zodiac was kept in his garden, and although humping it over the soft sand to the water's edge was always a laborious affair, Bob had devised a way of making it easier. This involved attaching to the transom of the inflatable two brackets, each fitted with a large spherical wheelbarrow wheel which was bright red in colour. Everybody in Beach House referred to them as 'Bob's Balls'. To the accompaniment of a fusillade of ribald comments Bob soon had his balls in position. A group of willing volunteers quickly hauled the boat and engine down the beach between recumbent sunbathers while I carried my heavy diving equipment to the water's edge. With a male labour force in wetsuits to assist, launching the boat into the gentle swell was no problem. We were soon skimming across the waves towards Godrevy Island, propelled by Bob's new engine.

We found Percy by a fishing boat, but the dolphin did not come to greet us until we made a close pass. There were no jubilant leaps. Still confident that my aquaplane would work the magic I slid overboard and was towed near the fishing boat. The Hydro-fin worked perfectly, especially under-water where it was much easier to control than my home-made aquaplane. I glided down and skimmed across the canopy of kelp that covered the sea bed, directing it up and down and from side to side. It felt like an underwater switchback ride. I loved it, and I felt Percy would too. I looked around expecting to see the dolphin swimming excitedly alongside. But there was no sign of him.

Seeing how much I had enjoyed myself, Geoffrey and Animal both had tows on the Hydro-fin, but Percy would have nothing to do with either of them. As long as we stayed in his territory the dolphin would occasionally pass close by the boat. But he showed none of the exuberant behaviour they had both seen earlier at first hand.

I suggested to Bob that we should try the one tactic that Donald, Jean Louis and Percy found irresistible. We put the folding anchor over the side and rattled it. Then we let it fall to the sea bed and heaved on the rope so that the chain attached to the anchor rattled on the rocks. But even that failed to elicit a spark of response from the sad, withdrawn dolphin.

My activities with the rope were so vigorous that the anchor slipped into a crevice in the rocks and jammed. We tried the usual methods of freeing it by moving the boat and tugging. But it remained firmly fixed.

'You'll have to put your bottle on, go down and free it,' said Bob.

I quickly hauled the harness of my aqualung over my shoulder and went down. After I had freed the anchor I rattled it and then tapped the anchor and the rocks with my knife handle. Percy did not come to me. I surfaced beside the boat. Bob hauled up the anchor and noticed Percy on the surface about two hundred yards away.

'Hang on to the side, Horace, I'll tow you over to him,' said Bob as he started the engine.

I clung to the hand rope and was hauled through the water towards the place where Percy had last surfaced. It was in the strait and a current was running. I let go, and could just see the dolphin with his head facing into the current at the limit of visibility. Even then he didn't come and say hello. I tried very hard to project to the dolphin a feeling of concern, calm and gentleness as I let myself drift towards him in the current, but he was nervous and swam away. As Percy sped past me I saw that a tangled ball of fishing line was hooked into his head. I had only a fleeting glimpse and could not tell if the hook was embedded in the eye or near by. In an instant Percy's change of behaviour was explained. Bob had been right after all. Percy was injured, but not by a propeller. With a hook embedded in his head, it was no wonder that he was nervous of humans and disinclined to perform acrobatics.

Everyone was very sad when I broke the news, and the film-show I put on for the guests at Beach House that evening was not the convivial event it should have been. We debated how the accident had happened. It is well accepted among anglers that sharks and other predatorial fish will take wounded or hooked fish. Indeed, the practice of live baiting for pike, for instance, is based on this instinctive behaviour. It is also widely known that dolphins are too intelligent to behave in this way. Percy had had many opportunities to take a snack when Bob was out jigging for mackerel, but he had never attempted to snatch a hooked fish. We dismissed the possibility that anyone would be foolish enough deliberately to hook Percy. So we came to the conclusion that Percy had been hooked accidentally, probably by a rod-and-line fisherman.

We then discussed how to help Percy. One suggestion was that we should capture him, surgically remove the hook, dress the wound and return the dolphin to the sea. I was firmly opposed to this course of action, for several reasons. First was the not inconsiderable difficulty of capturing a 700-pound dolphin without causing further, perhaps more serious, injuries. Second, even if we captured Percy without additional physical damage, there was a distinct risk that the stress of being restrained would lead to his death. Even if we were successful and did so with the best possible motives, I felt that hauling the dolphin out of the sea would irreparably damage Percy's friendly attitude to humans. Finally I argued that whenever possible, the natural repair and healing processes should be left to proceed unhindered. I was able to support my case by reference to Donald, who was shot twice, run over by a power boat, and had several major wounds inflicted upon him. Yet he recovered spontaneously, with apparently no long-term ill effects. However, I suggested that we should keep the situation under constant review. To do this we needed to observe Percy's behaviour and monitor his state of health as best we could.

At breakfast the next morning Bob told me that he had slept badly. He was worried about Percy and kept waking up and thinking about him. Immediately after breakfast we launched the Zodiac. As we thudded across the quiet sea towards Godrevy Island we gave one of the guests from Beach House a crash course on boat handling, as we wanted him to look after the inflatable while both Bob and I were under-water.

Well before we got to the island Percy came slicing through the water to greet us. He didn't come as close to the inflatable as he had a few weeks before, but we were all immensely relieved to see him, especially when he followed us into the quiet waters of Fisherman's Cove. We dropped the anchor overboard near a small pinnacle of rock remarkably like a smaller version of Dolphin Rock off the coast of Brittany. At irregular intervals a large wave would climb over the rocks at the foot of the island and form a cascading waterfall of white foam as it poured into the trough that followed. I looked down through the clear green water and could see roads of sand twisting their way through kelp-covered rocks. For a few moments the grey torpedo shape of Percy hung suspended like a shadow beneath the boat. Then he moved slowly and silently away.

Bob and I slid quietly into the water and descended to the sea bed. Percy made three or four fleeting passes at speed and disappeared. Bob and I swam round the island but saw no sign of him. We surfaced, and Bob climbed back aboard, saying he would go and look for Percy, who might have gone off feeding. I wanted to get some under-water pictures of Percy if I possibly could, so I stayed in the water to await Bob's return, hopefully with Percy alongside. As Bob accelerated away towards the open sea I went back to explore the undersea gulleys around the island.

As I approached I caught a glimpse of Percy, who must have been near us all the time but wished to remain unseen. I decided there was no point in attempting to swim after him because he was not interested in play – otherwise he would have taken off with Bob. He was also clearly nervous of humans. I decided it was best to remain very calm. That way Percy might gain sufficient confidence to approach a little closer. I meandered gently round the rocks, and Percy stayed with me for half an hour, swimming slowly past but never showing the bright curiosity which had been a characteristic of our earlier encounters, and upon which I depended to get my pictures. During one of his passes I saw a white strip of skin and epidermal tissue streaming from his eye, but no sign of the tangled ball of nylon line. I deduced that he had managed to get rid of the embedded hook, probably by rubbing against a rock, and in doing so had ripped his skin. Even if dislodging the hook had been a painful process I felt sure the dolphin experienced considerable relief as soon as the source of irritation and possible infection was removed. The water flowing past would flush the cut. Now it was up to Nature to heal the wound, as it did when dolphins sometimes raked one another with their teeth during courtship. How long this would take, and how much longer it would take Percy to restore his faith in those who went into the sea to seek his company, were unanswerable questions.

Bob returned while I was having my reunion with Percy and cruised gently around in the inflatable as I attempted, without success, to get close-up pictures of the wound. When I eventually surfaced, after spending a further ten minutes under-water without seeing Percy, Bob said, 'I think he really has gone off fishing this time.'

Geoffrey Lakeman, the *Daily Mirror* reporter, had arranged to take his family to Fisherman's Cove. After my swim with Percy we took the inflatable to the beach, where his children were put aboard, and set off in search of the dolphin.

We found him in his old territory near Godrevy Island and once again he raced towards us as we drew near. He swam around the boat, but declined to jump. Although he still seemed subdued and there were no opportunities to take more exciting pictures showing him leaping, Percy did follow us part-way back to Portreath, and I felt the crisis was over, that Percy would recover. This was the message I took to James Wharram when I left Portreath the same evening to put on a film show at the Dolphin Link Centre.

My film-lecture presentations have proved to be extremely valuable ways of drawing together people with an interest in dolphins, and sometimes with a special knowledge of their occurrence and habits. This applies particularly to the boating community, many of whom have encounters with dolphins which are not recorded, except perhaps in the ship's log. I have found that without exception they are pleased to discuss what they have seen with somebody like me who takes an interest and can perhaps supplement their observations. This was certainly the case the first time we gathered in Devoran to set up the Dolphin Link Project. Then Dick Lightfoot, a local sailor who ran a flotilla of charter yachts, showed me a chart on which he had plotted numerous dolphin sightings.

A similar situation applied after I left Portreath following the unfortunate incident with Percy and the fishing line. On Saturday, 24 September, I gave a dolphin film-show at the Oasis Palace in Marbella, to raise money for Aspandem, a charitable organisation devoted to the care of mentally handicapped children in Spain. Numerous boat-owners attended the gala evening, and they told me that the coast, along the south-eastern tip of Spain from Almería to Algeciras, was patrolled throughout the year by schools of dolphins. One of the people who came to the show was a friend, Mike Lawrence, who had turned this concentration of dolphins to his advantage in Gibraltar where he ran dolphin safaris from Shephard's Marina. Although it was a commercial operation I felt Mike did a wonderful job as a dolphin ambassador. He dearly loved the dolphins he took his paying passengers out to see each day on *Sea Marauder*. The dolphins got to know the sound of his engine and would swim between the hulls of the catamaran. Those passengers bold enough to lie on the deck between the hulls could sometimes touch the dorsal fins of the dolphins that chose, of their own free will, to escort *Sea Marauder* on her sightseeing cruises. Each one of these dolphin watchers became an instant dolphin conservationist, and these meetings with free-ranging wild dolphins in the Straits of Gibraltar were one of their most cherished memories.

Prior to giving my show in Marbella I was taken by my hostess, Annabelle Pluck, to Banus where I saw the bleeding corpses of sharks hanging on the jetty. I openly expressed my opposition to the barbaric practice of shark-fishing during my presentation at the Oasis Palace. Knowing of the considerable commercial interest in shark-fishing as a tourist attraction, I expected to be booed at this point. Much to my surprise, however, I received a spontaneous round of applause. I was approached by one of the major shark fishermen who admitted that he had got bored with routine trips which entailed hours at sea, during which most of his passengers became seasick, and very few actually caught sharks. None the less he had a great love of the sea and enjoyed making a living by taking people out in his boat. During his shark-fishing trips he had unwittingly gained a considerable knowledge of the habits of the dolphins, who often followed him during parts of his journeys to and from the deep offshore waters where he trolled for sharks. He said he had never considered taking out passengers on dolphin-watching trips. When I told him that whale-watching was big business in the United States he said he would look into dolphin-watching as an alternative to shark-fishing. I wished him success if he changed.

I already knew of the abundance of dolphins in the area because friends of Annabelle Pluck asked me to go out dolphin-spotting on their yacht. During an afternoon cruise we found several schools of Common dolphins. From their behaviour I could see that most of them were feeding. Even so, they would break off from their meal to frolic in the bow wave until we went over an invisible boundary line. Once we did that they would all move away. Despite the fact that the sea was calm and there were as many as thirty or forty dolphins in a school, it was easy to lose them at this stage.

We stopped the boat several times, and some of the passengers jumped in with snorkelling equipment to swim with the dolphins. When the snorkellers put their heads under-water they could hear the sounds of the dolphins very clearly and got fleeting glimpses of them through the translucent water. But the dolphins would not allow contact and usually moved away after a few minutes.

The Common dolphin (*Delphinus delphis*) is a much more nervous species than the Bottlenose dolphin (*Tursiops truncatus*). Thus I did not expect them to be quite as friendly as a school to which Donald, Jean Louis or Percy might have belonged. Even so, they did imbue all those aboard, and those in the water, with a joyous feeling which contrasted very strongly with the fear and horror many had experienced when they saw sharks.

My dolphin-watching cruise off the Costa del Sol was most enjoyable, but it did make me aware once again just how fortunate I had been to have swum with not just one but two friendly wild dolphins a few weeks earlier. Furthermore, Percy and Jean Louis were probably the only two dolphins in the world at that time to prefer the company of humans to that of their own kind on a long-term basis. Now I was anxious to go back to Portreath and see if I could make contact with Percy again before winter set in.

Within a week of returning home I was able to travel to Portreath via Harrow, where I gave another film-show, this time on making underwater movies, at the College of Art. My lecture visit to the West Country also took in Lynmouth, which at night was as romantic as a film set, the lights on the steep surrounding streets reflected in the tumbling waters of the River Lyn adding to the magic of a still, end-of-summer evening.

Animal, the press photographer, was also keen to renew his friendship with Percy. We arranged to meet in Portreath together with some Australian friends who had organised lectures for me in Sydney and were keen to meet the friendly wild dolphin. We were all disappointed, however, because the summer was over. We had missed it by one day.

We climbed up the steep cliff-path to the top of Ralph's Cupboard where we were buffeted by gale-force onshore winds. Beneath us the angry sea pounded the cliffs. Frenzied waves tossed spume into the air and the wind carried it to the top of the cliff where it drenched us. It was a powerful, awe-inspiring sight and we all knew that somewhere out on the roaring sea was a lonely dolphin. Would he ride out the tempest and stay? Or would he move on to warmer, more hospitable climes?

We didn't know.

Back at Beach House we discussed the possibilities with Bob who said that he would attempt to maintain contact with Percy. During spells of calm weather he would take his inflatable, with its new reliable engine, out round the Stones off Godrevy Island, because that was where he was convinced Percy would be found if the dolphin decided to remain off Cornwall throughout the oncoming winter.

· 9 ·

Dolphin Intelligence

Winter is a depressing time for many in the West Country. At the end of the summer the pleasure boats are wisely taken from their moorings and waterfront kiosks are boarded up to protect them from the gales that howl in from the Atlantic. The winds whip the sea into a frenzy before venting their fury on anything in their paths when they come ashore. There are also long periods when the weather is grey, damp and monotonously miserable. These are interspersed at totally unpredictable intervals by glorious sunny calm spells that instantly dispel the winter gloom.

It was during one of these welcome respites at the end of November, 1983, that James Wharram decided to see if he could find Percy. He took the Humber inflatable, which had given such good service in Brittany, to the north coast of Cornwall and set out for Godrevy Island. Ruth Wharram was one of the passengers, and in a letter to me she described what happened when they reached the far side of the island. From the direction of the Stones Percy came bounding across the sea. The dolphin seemed as delighted to see those on the inflatable as they undoubtedly were to see him, circling round them and doing some leaps. Then he tried to draw the Dolphin Link group further out towards the reef. James had great faith in sailing ships, but never fully trusted engines. With a strong offshore wind blowing he did not want to risk an engine failure, for without power, even with oars, he knew he would be blown out to sea. So he headed back towards the shore, and much to his delight Percy followed, performing a couple of spectactular leaps on the way. They passed through the discoloured water at the river mouth, then James put on a mask and slipped over the side. The visibility under-water was poor and James could not see Percy's eye clearly enough to inspect it. However, from the dolphin's friendly behaviour, James concluded that he was in good spirits. Ruth's letter put me in good spirits too, because I was concerned that even if the injuries to Percy by the fishing-line incident had not seriously harmed him they might have prompted the dolphin to move elsewhere.

The winter months are usually a hectic period for me, because that is the time when many people with outdoor interests go indoors for their entertainment. This can take the form of lectures and film-shows, which I provide. The winter of 1983–4 was no exception, with a lecture tour in the United States as well as presentations in every corner of Britain. I thoroughly enjoy giving lectures. First, because I like to tell people about the magic of dolphins, and secondly because they sometimes trigger off a chain of events that have the most surprising outcome for me at a time and place far removed from the lecture hall. For example, it was as a direct result of a film-show at Hout Bay in 1978, when I launched International Dolphin Watch in South Africa, that Annabelle Pluck contacted me and asked me to give a film presentation in Marbella. Similarly, when I spoke at a ladies' luncheon club in Ipswich in March, 1983, I had no idea that one of the books I signed after my speech would find its way to Arabia, and that this would lead directly to my being invited by Alex Collett, an English business entrepreneur who worked for an Arab sheik, to give a film show in Abu Dhabi in April, 1984.

Prior to my arrival in Abu Dhabi I assumed that as a result of the enormous changes, including a considerable amount of drilling and dredging, the offshore life would be sparse. Much to my surprise and delight, however, I found it to be prolific – especially the bird life. I saw flamingoes; and one small island, which looked from afar as if it was covered with black tar, turned out to be a resting place for thousands of cormorants which took to the air when a speedboat passed by. Indeed, it was while going to have a look at an osprey perched on a post on the side of a channel that I discovered a small school of Humpback dolphins (*Sousa chinensis*), so called because their recurved dorsal fins are perched on the tops of distinct humps. Pale grey in colour, they were about six feet long. They appeared to disregard our boat, taking no notice of me when I was towed at the end of a rope through their midst. Unfortunately, underwater visibility was limited to about four feet and I caught only glimpses of them as I was trolled back and forth across the channel in which they were feeding. Indeed, I gained a greater knowledge of what they were doing from my above-water observations.

It was fascinating to see how they worked as a hunting pack. From their movements when they surfaced it was obvious that they were rounding up fish and herding them into a ball. The trick then was to attempt gently to ease the boat to where you thought the fish would be corraled. When this happened the dolphins would rush into them and for a few minutes there would be a burst of turmoil on the surface, with dolphins zooming around in all directions. Then suddenly, they would all vanish, presumably as the fish dispersed. The round-up would start again perhaps two to three hundred yards away.

As they hunt in water where the visibility is always low these dolphins must depend mostly on echo-location to find their prey. But do they use sonar beams to form sonic fences? Or do the dolphins work like silent sheepdogs using the physical presence of their bodies to frighten the fish into swimming where they want them to? I dearly wanted to put a hydrophone into the water and listen to their sounds, and perhaps one day I will have an opportunity to go back and do so. If I return I would also like to investigate reports that many dolphins follow the old dhow trading routes from the Persian Gulf into the Indian Ocean on migrations that appear to take place annually.

My film lecture, which was billed as a DOLPHIN SPECTA-
CULAR in Abu Dhabi, attracted a big audience, many of
whom had boats. At the end of my presentation I asked the
boat owners to mark on a chart pinned up in the foyer
where they had seen dolphins. I was thereby able to conduct
an instant dolphin survey of the area.

With the help of Alex Collett, who took me out in his
speedboat with his delightful family, and the Abu Dhabi
Branch of the British Sub-Aqua Club, who put a boat and a
voluntary crew at my disposal, I was able to cover a large
sea area myself. It was during a visit to a zone marked with
lots of crosses on my survey chart that I came across the
osprey and the feeding dolphins.

During my one-week stay in Abu Dhabi many of the
divers became enthusiastic dolphin spotters and wanted to
continue to study the dolphins after I left. I therefore
drafted and agreed a proposal for a research project which
would involve the joint participation of the Sub-Aqua Club
and the Natural History Group. I defined the aims and
objectives of the project as follows:

> The project will provide valuable insight into the little
> known behaviour of dolphins as a social group. It will
> also provide essential background information against
> which changes in population and behaviour can be
> monitored in a sea area which is being subjected to major
> changes as a result of the dredging operations and
> waterfront developments linked with the rapid expan-
> sion of Abu Dhabi.
>
> Eventually it is hoped that experienced observers will
> take out parties of schoolchildren and interested adults
> on special excursions to see dolphins in their natural
> habitat. The situation will provide an alternative to
> seeing dolphins in captivity. During the boat trips
> emphasis will be made on the need to behave in a sensible
> manner when in the company of the dolphins, which
> should not be harassed. Such excursions should also
> indicate sightings of the rich wildlife associated with the

channels. These include many spectacular and beautiful birds such as ospreys, flamingoes, cormorants and terns. The excursions can be part of an overall programme of education which hopefully will inspire a love of all wildlife associated with the sea. This should lead, in turn, to a spontaneous desire to conserve the rich wildlife heritage of Abu Dhabi.

Everyone was happy with the first proposal. The second, however, was controversial and a number of people expressed concern that boatloads of trippers would damage the wildlife by harassment. I argued that overall experience does not bear this out and quoted the case of the increase in popularity of birdwatching in Britain, where a relatively small group has aroused an interest in birds in a much larger percentage of the population, who in their turn have appreciated the need for conservation and have acted accordingly. As a result, some bird habitats have been protected and others created specifically for the purpose. An example is the increased number of migratory geese that now winter in East Anglia and flourish during their stay partly because of the food supplement in the form of surplus potatoes provided by the birdwatchers. Thus the birds have benefited from being watched, and many humans have enjoyed seeing them directly through binoculars, or indirectly via television programmes.

I saw dolphin-watching as a logical progression from birdwatching, and a step towards my wish to see an end to the capture of dolphins for display in dolphinariums. This in turn was consistent with my deep-felt, long-term desire to see human society moving towards a state where there would be much greater harmony and intimate co-existence between humans and all forms of wildlife. I knew that such an attitude ran counter to man's trend towards absolute control over his environment and all the life forms on the planet. It was for human convenience and entertainment that we kept birds and most large animals in cages. In my view, television had a far greater educational value than seeing a bedraggled animal pacing back and forth in a confined space. This was especially true for people whose economic or physical circumstances prohibited expensive travel. However, I felt that those who wanted to see live animals should be encouraged to do so, in their natural environment.

I have a deep-rooted feeling for the freedom of all creatures. On reflection I suspect that one of the subconscious reasons for my obsessive interest in Jean Louis and Percy was that they embodied a spirit of freedom very close to my heart. Dolphins are not constrained by the codes of conduct that demand control of feelings and constraint of open expressions of emotion. If Percy wanted to jump for joy, he did so. If he wanted to be quiet on his own, he could do so. If he wanted to associate with humans and enjoy their company, he could do so.

Many people long for this kind of freedom, and I attempted to express it in a poem I wrote immediately after I met him in 1982.

> Pushing through green waters
> Symbol of joy
> You leap from the depths
> To touch the sky
> Scattering spray like handfuls of jewels.
>
> Not caged by union rules
> Unfettered by sales targets
> No trains, or planes to catch
> Your time is set by the flow
> Of the sea's tide
> And the moon's glow.
>
> You give us images of ecstasy
> That we lock away
> Behind the doors of memory
> For quiet moments
> When released by our possessions
> We dream of freedom like yours.

I knew I was exceptionally fortunate to be in a position

where I could organise my life in such a way that I could pursue my dolphin interests and earn a living at the same time. Thus I arranged to put on a film-show in the village hall in Devoran immediately after Easter, 1984. This would enable me to meet James Wharram and find out how the Dolphin Link Project was progressing. A second film-show at a regional meeting of Women's Institutes in Perranporth justified a diversion to see Bob and Judy Holborn and catch up on the latest news on Percy.

Eleven days after my return from Abu Dhabi I drove once again into the drive at Beach House in Portreath. Bob and Judy were both out when I arrived, so I chatted to the Ward family, regular visitors to Portreath from their home in North Yorkshire with whom I had become friendly. The first news they told me was that while I had been giving my talk in the village hall the previous evening Percy had come into the bay at Portreath. Everyone was naturally delighted because the fishermen said they had not seen the dolphin for months. However, the Wards knew Percy was still in the vicinity because he had come to Bob's boat a few weeks previously. There was no sign of the hook near the dolphin's eye. The Wards' eleven-year-old daughter, Joanna, told me that the highlight of her summer holiday in 1983 was going out with Bob to see Percy. She then coyly showed me a cuddly dolphin she had made and which she wanted to show to its model, the real Percy.

I was told that Bob had gone out in his inflatable to see if he could find Percy and that Judy had driven to Godrevy to watch from the shore. We decided to climb the cliffs to see if we could spot Percy from the high vantage point.

It was a crisp spring day, with a brisk wind. The Ward family were each wearing a navy-blue pullover with a leaping dolphin boldly displayed in white on the front. The waxy-yellow cups of clusters of Lesser celandines shone in the dark green foliage along the damp edge of the narrow pathway that led up to the top of the towering cliffs beside Beach House. Near the summit a herd of Friesian cows used their tongues to scythe the field in which they were confined. They raised their heads as we approached and stood watching us, noisily munching the juicy new grass. Above us the song of the skylarks tumbled out of the blue heavens. As there was no sign of Percy we walked on to a second headland.

An inflatable with four divers aboard came into view from the direction of Godrevy. It dropped anchor near the foot of the cliffs and two divers went overboard. We gazed down on them, knowing that if Percy was near he would come to investigate. As the dolphin did not surface we assumed he was at Godrevy and turned back for home.

On our way back we saw a black fishing boat with a white wheelhouse and the registration PZ127 clearly painted on the side. Through my binoculars I watched the crew pulling in their pots over the bows. Circling round the centre of activity was Percy. I recognised his characteristic behaviour. He would watch something with rapt attention for a few seconds, during which time he remained still. Then, with sudden flick of his tail, he would twist round, dive, and reappear somewhere else.

Just as the last pot was pulled aboard, the inflatable full of divers came into view and Percy disappeared. So too did the inflatable as it went round the headland towards Portreath. Leaving the others to walk back to Beach House I ran to the top of the headland to see if Percy was following the red inflatable. There was a very strong wind blowing, and when I reached the summit I could see the heavily laden boat thumping into the waves and sending up clouds of spray that drenched those aboard, who were all wearing diving suits. I could hear the shout of delight when they discovered they had a dolphin for company. As soon as they were out of the very rough water off the headland three divers fell off the side of the inflatable like ninepins.

From my vantage point on top of the cliffs I was much more aware of where Percy was and what he was doing than any of the divers. The three in the water were all distinctively different. One wore a red drysuit, another a blue drysuit and the third a black suit. Percy visited all of them in turn but had a definite preference for the man in blue. Percy often swam unseen just a few inches behind a snorkel diver who was swimming vigorously and searching everywhere for the apparently elusive dolphin. Then Percy would accelerate past the astonished swimmer in an open invitation to play tag.

A small leap near the boat would have all three divers finning as fast as they could towards the spot where Percy submerged. But inevitably by the time they arrived the dolphin was somewhere else. When Alan Vine's little boat, which had been smartly painted during the winter months, came chugging out of the harbour Percy left the divers. For a brief time the dolphin did a spell of escort duty. But when the *Tar dor Moor* went wallowing round the headland Percy returned to the divers, who were all too willing to continue to play with him. The boathandler eventually cut the engine and joined in the fun. The divers all stayed close to the red inflatable which was being driven out to sea by the increasing offshore wind.

I sat for an hour in a cosy nook out of the wind on the cliff-top watching the divers and the dolphin enjoying themselves together. In their dry suits they were warm and dry, and despite the fact that they were surrounded by large white-capped waves they were quite safe, because at any time they could scramble back to the inflatable which bobbed like a cork near by. When Percy decided it was time to end the game he swiftly vanished. I didn't see him go. Nor did the divers.

When the divers climbed back aboard their Humber inflatable I decided to get an account of their feelings towards Percy. I walked down the cliffs, across the beach, and arrived at the harbour just as they were hauling the boat up the slipway. The leader of the group, Trevor, recognised me and introduced me to the others, who said how exciting it had been. They had all wanted to touch Percy, but at the moment they thought their hands would make contact the dolphin managed to move away, just out of range. They also commented on how Percy came 'to look them in the eye', approaching to within a few feet before swimming quickly away. They confirmed that although Percy had many scars there was no sign of an injury close to either of his eyes.

I told them that I was showing my film of Donald that night in Perranporth and suggested they might like to join the ladies from the Women's Institutes.

As I made my way back across the beach the holiday-makers who had come to catch the late April sunshine were packing up and trekking back home. I sat on a rock and was mesmerised by the sound of the surf as the wind pulled off the tops of the waves in plumes of spume that followed the crests like white feathers on a helmet. The sun still shone out of a cloudless sky. Sometimes it would catch the wind-blown spray on the top of a wave, and for a brief moment a rainbow would form.

Bob and Judy were still not back when I set off to give my film-show at the Memorial Hall in Perranporth. I left a message inviting them and their guests to attend, having confirmed with the organiser that she would not object to having a party of dolphin-loving gatecrashers.

It was one of those shows I remember with great affection. The lady in charge was extremely nervous, but she introduced me delightfully with a Cornish accent and local expressions which I found captivating. The Holborns and their guests arrived shortly after I began my talk but the four divers, who were all from the Birmingham area, turned up early. In addition to watching my film they sat through the entire Women's Institute meeting, which included judging the best scotch egg, a floral art competition, a home-made wine tasting and numerous other items on a long agenda, which was quickly covered because the meeting was efficiently organised and run. One of the divers, a social worker in the heart of Birmingham, said that for him the entire evening was a wonderful experience. He had heard of the W.I., of course, but he had had no idea what happy gatherings their meetings were,

14-15 Percy enjoyed racing along with the catamaran (*above*), as well as cavorting with those who jumped into the sea when it anchored (*below*).

16 The warm weather enabled the Dolphin Link group to enjoy their Polynesian life-style.
17 Carola Hepp beside the mural she designed and painted at the Dolphin Link base in Devoran.

nor what an important role they obviously played in the social life of rural communities.

When we eventually got back to Beach House Judy apologised and told me the reason for their late arrival at Perranporth was because Percy had decided to put on a dolphin show in the bay just as they were about to leave. So they waited until his show was over before coming on to mine. Bob then told me that the winter had been the worst he had ever known and described what it must have been like on the Stones during the fiercest gales. He didn't find it at all surprising when Percy appeared bearing many new scars.

Joanna's father, a medical practitioner, asked me to expand further on the subject of the dolphin brain and intelligence which I had raised during my talk to the W.I. in Perranporth. I was happy to do so because it was a subject that fascinated me. Furthermore, I was developing a new theory in which I postulated that the brain was like a computer and that intelligence could be likened to a computer program.

Part of my monologue went as follows:

The number of functions a computer will perform is directly related to its memory, the capacity of which is measured in bytes; the larger the computer, the greater is its capability. I suggest that each of these bytes could be likened to the basic units, or neurones, in the brain. The greater the brain size, the more complex are the functions it can perform. As a child grows its brain size increases and it develops intelligence.

When a child is born it cries spontaneously when stimulated by pain, discomfort and hunger. These are reflex reactions that do not require thought processes. However, it cannot walk, it cannot talk, and it cannot solve problems. An ability to do these things is very slowly acquired through learning processes in which messages received from different parts of the body are transmitted to the brain via nerves. In the brain the impulses are processed in such a way that the child becomes aware of a specific situation. If you like, this can be regarded as the input to the computer. The next phase is for the brain to process that information and initiate a train of reactions in response to the input. For instance, when a child smells food, hears it being put on to a plate, and then sees it set on a tray, it has an input into the auditory (hearing) component, the olfactory (smell) component and the visual components of its brain. These signals are then processed and orders are sent out to begin the complex task of transferring the food, little by little, to the buccal cavity (mouth). Those who have studied the mess a one-year-old baby gets into when attempting to shovel food into its mouth will appreciate what a complex manipulative process it is. At this stage the higher levels of the brain, the cerebral cortex, have only a minor role.

Gradually, however, as more and more of what we think of as the simpler tasks are mastered, the cerebral cortex plays a more and more important role. By the time the child reaches five, great advances in physical co-ordination have been made. At that age a child may respond to music but will not appreciate the subtleties of Mozart and will not be able to comprehend concepts as complex as water evaporating and then condensing to steam. It takes a further five to ten years of brain growth and learning for this to happen. Not until the child reaches adulthood will it appreciate a candle-lit dinner, with musical accompaniment, spent with a companion. At that stage it will be the higher centres of the brain, the cerebral cortex, that are playing a major role and will ultimately result in a feeling of well-being which is far removed from the basic desire to eat solely in order to survive. Although we all think we quite spontaneously appreciate the subtleties of soft lights and sweet music we would not be able to do so without a large brain or without undergoing the learning process during which the higher levels of our brains have been frequently stimulated. In order to reach this level we have had to solve lots of problems on the way, which means we have had to develop our intelligence. Without large brains with big cerebral cortices we would not be intelligent.

Bottlenose dolphins have brains as big as those of humans, and archaeological evidence indicates that they have been endowed with them for millions of years longer than us. Although the overall shape of a modern Bottlenose dolphin's brain is different from that of a human, internal regions associated with reception and interpretation of signals from various senses can be identified. Thus, as is to be expected, the dolphin's auditory centre is larger than that of a human, whereas the olfactory lobes are very small. However, the cerebral cortex is as large as that of a human and its surface is even more complex and convoluted. It is widely accepted that neurones in this surface layer are involved with higher mental processes.

I support the view that if the large complex cerebral cortex of the dolphin were not fulfilling an important role evolutionary progress would have caused it to atrophy over a period of millions of years. Thus it can be argued that the dolphins are likely to have evolved even higher thought processes than humans because the need to deploy most of their mental resources to feeding themselves and surviving in a hostile environment was removed millions of years ago, whereas in evolutionary terms, humans have only very recently reached this stage on a global scale. This brings us to the question of precisely what does go on in a brain large enough to have thought processes as complex as and perhaps even more highly evolved than our own.

Being non-manipulative creatures dolphins do not have art, music, literature and diversely processed food to generate the very subtle differences in sensory inputs that make us feel good when we hear moving music, or see a beautiful painting. It is my view, however, that they are equally able to differentiate tiny changes in often very complex sensory inputs. They experience feelings akin to those of aesthetic pleasure in humans, not from music or art, but from subtleties of their environment, such as sounds of the sea on a distant shore, or the interplay of light on the kelp in an undersea canyon. To appreciate them they do not have to rationalise them as I have done, just as we don't have to know how an electronic organ works in order to appreciate the sounds it produces.

In this way I can account for the habit shared by Percy and Jean Louis of swimming close to the propellers of boats. These would create vast numbers of pressure waves that would dance over the surface of the dolphin's skin generating touch sensations. These would probably not be too far removed from those experienced by Jean Louis when she was in very rough water – which we called her jacuzzi – an experience she learned to appreciate in her formative years.

To conclude my monologue to the captive audience at Beach House I said that dolphins have brains or computers as big as ours. They therefore have a potential as great as ours for higher level thought processes. But their intelligence, that is their computer programs, was completely different from ours, as if written in a different computer language.

I wanted to attempt to bridge the gap between the human computer and the dolphin computer, and to do that I needed to find in what language the dolphin's computer program was written. In other words, I wanted to find out how a dolphin thinks.

To go beyond what I had achieved with Jean Louis I needed to establish a much closer relationship with Percy. The first step along this road would be to get to the stage where Percy would allow prolonged direct physical contact with a human. As I had to leave the following morning it was up to Bob to provide a continuity of human friendship with Percy. This I was absolutely sure he would do.

A few days later, when he was at Godrevy Point looking

out for Percy, Bob saw a lady standing on the headland calling out, 'Donald, Donald' over the water. This was what I had done to call up the dolphin at the beginning of the film I showed at Perranporth. Realising what she was trying to do, Bob went up behind her and said, 'Excuse me, it's not Donald, it's Percy.'

The lady turned round and said, 'Oh, you must be Bob from Portreath.'

She said she was disappointed because she couldn't see the dolphin. Then Percy popped up. Bob pointed him out and gave her his binoculars. He also directed her vision to the seals which were in the water. She was overwhelmed.

When Bob left she again started calling out, 'Donald, Donald' over the water.

'Ah, so much for human intelligence,' Bob sighed to himself.

The Magic of Dolphins

The publication of a new book is an exciting time. Launch date for my book, *The Magic of Dolphins*, was fixed for 6 June, 1984 – the thirtieth anniversary of the D-Day landings in Europe.

That Wednesday was also a D-Day for me, but in this case D signified Dolphin. After the launch in London I travelled via Bristol to Devoran to do a television interview aboard the *Teheni*, which was moored outside the Dolphin Link Headquarters. I was greeted with affection, as always, by Ruth Wharram, but she was obviously distressed and I soon discovered why. She had heard that a dead dolphin had been washed up near Godrevy and it sounded very much as if it was Percy. Ruth then showed me a report. It was in childish writing and had been given to her by Nicola Barrett, a local schoolgirl who had attended one of my lectures. Here is exactly how Nicola described the body on the beach:

> The dolphin was first found on St Ives bay, then it moved round to Hayle beach then to where I live (Gwithian).
>
> It was a bottle-nose-dolphin, it was 12–13 feet long, it had been shot near the base of its tail. His eyes had gone (both) and his mouth was open and it had blood on its teeth. It had been dead about two weeks, and you know that their belly is white, this one's belly was turning purple and you could see what it had been eating. It had lots of cuts, scars, and bruises on its body.

Underneath the neatly written paragraphs was the laconic phrase 'Here it is', with an arrow pointing to a stark drawing illustrating a dead dolphin with a damaged dorsal fin. A feature not mentioned in her report was a bullet wound, which was very clearly indicated.

The film crew were already present when I arrived, and I was soon sitting on the deck of the *Teheni* telling an interviewer about the magic of dolphins.

I told him the book was so-called because dolphins appear to have the qualities that most of us would like to see in our fellow humans. These extend to being unaggressive even when subjected to pain and threatened with death. With the almost unthinkable prospect of Percy being shot hovering in my mind, I thought it extremely unlikely that I would be tempted to write a book about the magic of my own species.

As soon as the camera crew had packed up I drove to Portreath to find out what the Holborns knew.

Judy told me the full story, which had started for her on Friday, 1 June. On her way to Godrevy to do some Percy-watching she had called in at the National Trust hut to get a ticket. When she mentioned she had come to see Percy the ticket man replied, 'Oh, you're wasting your time because he's been washed up dead.'

Judy was dumbfounded. 'What do you mean he's been washed up dead?' she replied, when she had recovered from the initial shock.

'Well, I tell you, I went down on the beach and had a look for myself. The dolphin was dead. And I've put a curse on the fishermen because I'm sure they did it.'

Four days had elapsed since the body, which had since been removed, was washed up on the beach near Godrevy Point. From the description, it sounded like Percy. Judy rushed home to tell Bob, who looked at her with disbelief. But when he thought back over the past week he realised he had not seen Percy for several days.

Bob had been studying Percy's habits and movements and had got to the stage where he could predict a rough daily timetable of activities for the dolphin. He knew, if other distractions were absent, that Percy would spend a couple of hours a day feeding near Godrevy Point at certain states of the tide. He looked at his watch and the tide tables.

'He should be feeding right now,' he said to Judy. 'I still don't think he's dead. I'm going to go and look for him.'

Bob drove to Godrevy Point and stayed there for a long time scanning the sea through binoculars, but Percy was nowhere to be seen. Unable to eat the sandwiches he had taken with him, Bob despondently returned home.

That night Judy woke up from a nightmare because she thought Percy was dead. So did Bob. They lay in bed talking as if they had lost a best friend. The truth might be terrible, but they wanted to know.

The next day they started making enquiries which led to several conflicting reports as to the precise day the body was first seen. This was very important, because Bob had been out and seen Percy alive and well on Sunday, 27 May, the same day that the National Trust man thought he had been down to the beach. Eventually they managed to make contact with the policeman to whom the incident had been officially notified. He came up with some precise information. The dead dolphin had been reported on Monday, 28 May; he also confirmed that the dolphin had been shot because there was a hole in its side about one-and-a-half inches in diameter and surrounded by what appeared to be pepper shot; the wound was still bleeding; the dolphin was black and had a white underbelly. Then he said the body was six to seven feet long, and that one fact gave Bob and Judy hope that it was not Percy, who with an estimated length of about twelve feet, was much bigger.

But the policeman had not seen the body. He only noted what had been reported to him. So how accurate was the report?

Eventually Judy tracked down one of the holiday-makers who had seen the corpse on the beach. She and her husband confirmed that the dolphin was about seven feet long and had a clear gunshot wound. They were also absolutely certain that they had seen the dead dolphin on Satur-

day, 26 May, because that was the first day of their holiday
and they had made their first stop at Godrevy.

This was sufficient for Bob and Judy to feel certain that
the dolphin washed up at Godrevy was not Percy. But that
being so – where was Percy?

They asked the fishermen they knew were friendly
towards Percy, and all confirmed that the dolphin had not
been seen for several days.

The next day, Sunday, 3 June, Bob went to Godrevy
Point but could find no indication of Percy's presence. Still
unwilling to believe that Percy would desert them, he and
Judy returned to the cliffs overlooking Godrevy Island the
following day. They scanned the sea through their binoculars, looking and hoping, but still saw no sign of the
dolphin. After about twenty minutes Bob said, 'Let's walk
down towards Portreath way and just look in the next bay.
He sometimes goes there.'

It was a nice day and they followed the coastal footpath.
When the next bay came into view they did not have to use
their binoculars to see a dolphin do a gentle roll. They stood
still, watching with joy. Of all the thousands – no, millions
– of dolphins in the world, they knew the one they were
watching was Percy. He was not dead after all.

When the full story was recounted to me we were all
concerned for Percy's future safety because we realised that
the body could very easily have been his.

I telephoned Ruth and told her that her fears were
unfounded, that I was going to stay overnight with the
Holborns and was looking forward to going out to see
Percy the next day. I accepted Ruth's kind invitation to
return to Devoran for an evening meal afterwards, and
promised to give her a full report on Percy's state of health.

I think it was Percy's recent reincarnation more than the
wine we consumed that made the evening I spent at Beach
House so enjoyable. Most of the time our conversation
centred on our friendly dolphin and the growing interest in
him from all quarters. As a result Bob and Judy were being
visited by an increasing number of people with a pro-

fessional interest in dolphins. One of them was a lady with whom I had a long-term friendly association, Dr Christina Lockyer, who was one of the very few professional scientists in the United Kingdom to make a fulltime living from research into whales and dolphins. Bob told me how he had taken her and a colleague to a vantage point on the top of the cliffs to video-tape Percy's behaviour when feeding. They filmed for two hours, without moving the camera, and stopped recording only when Percy suddenly vanished. I knew the scenario well. In my imagination I could see them happily watching Percy's every move until he had had his lunch, when he would disappear completely, without trace. A short time later he would appear, equally magically, in front of Beach House.

According to Bob, the dolphin had been making more frequent visits to Portreath before his disappearance at the time when the body was washed up at Godrevy. When I asked why he thought Percy had vanished, he replied, 'I just felt that Percy had obviously known something about the other dolphin being shot, and had just gone from the area.'

When I asked if the incident had affected the dolphin's behaviour, Bob told me that he had to go a long way out to sea in his inflatable to make contact. 'But now, having found him, he's started coming in and playing with the fishermen. He's got back to his old habits of following pots down when they're chucked in, and watching them when they're pulled up again,' he continued, 'so he comes in every day. Then he just vanishes – then there's no sign of him at all along the coast locally.'

Bob and Judy were having Beach House converted into two apartments. Before I went up the outside staircase to the newly transformed upper floor I asked Bob what the prospects were of seeing Percy the next day. When he said they were good I went to bed full of hope.

The next morning my hopes were shattered when I woke to see Portreath enveloped in dense fog. I could only just see the water's edge from the house. A very heavy surf thundered on to the beach. There was absolutely no possibility of going out in such conditions.

I waited until after midday for the fog to clear, but it didn't. So I set off for Devoran to see Ruth, who I knew would not object to my arriving early, especially if I was armed with a couple of bottles of wine. When I got to Redruth I burst through the fog into a brilliantly sunny June day.

James, Hanneke and the rest of the inmates at the Dolphin Link Centre were away in Holland, leaving Ruth and Carola to look after the base. Ruth prepared a splendid meal and Carola provided a post-prandial cabaret, singing some of the many songs she had composed and accompanying herself on the guitar. In her recital she included the song she wrote about another dolphin – Jean Louis. I had last heard it when sitting aboard the *Teheni* in La Baie des Trépassés, with Jean Louis as well as the camera crew for an audience.

The next morning was flawless – a white sun in a cloudless sky and no wind. Before I headed back to Portreath Carola showed me the many herbs she had planted in the beds she had cleared of scrub around the Dolphin Link Centre. Conditions looked ideal until I approached Portreath, where I plunged once again into a blanket of fog that muted the colours and lowered my spirits. However, it was not as thick as the previous day, and when I arrived Judy told me that Bob had gone to sea with the BBC cameraman, Jeff Goodman, with whom I had had a long and interesting conversation the previous day. They did not return until after lunch, when Bob informed me that Percy was in a lively mood. He had left the dolphin enjoying himself, playing around two fishing boats.

I helped Jeff unload his camera equipment, carrying the half-empty fuel can back to the garage at Beach House and returning with a new full can. Then, after helping Judy and Tricia Kirkman to board the inflatable, I pushed it forward into the gently breaking waves, and hauled myself aboard. Bob started the engine and we set off, but after about a hundred yards the engine juddered to a stop and refused to start. After tinkering with it, Bob and I decided it must be the new, untried fuel tank, so we rowed back to shore and I plodded up the beach again to recover the one I had just taken to the garage. I was hot and sticky inside my wetsuit by the time this operation was complete and I had again pushed the inflatable out into water deep enough to start the engine. Bob was anxious to get going as soon as possible because the tide was starting to run and that was the time Percy often went out to sea to feed. He did not want to go too far out to sea in foggy conditions with non-diving passengers aboard, especially when we were not sure about the reliability of the engine.

Judy noticed a small fishing boat close to the towering cliffs, and Bob recognised it as one of those that had claimed Percy's attention when he was out earlier. Even though we could see no sign of Percy through our binoculars we decided to investigate and headed for the boat, which was so dwarfed by the massive rockface that it looked like a toy. I was reduced to silence by the magnificence and beauty of the coastal scenery. A huge bank of bluebells spread like an eiderdown over part of the cliffs, seeming to glow softly from within, despite the overcast sky.

As we approched the boat there was still no sign of the dolphin. Then suddenly, a silver-grey arch formed briefly beside our boat. Although I did not photograph it, it etched an image in my memory as positive as a photograph. There was the lovely smiling face, the bright eyes and all the joy of Percy captured in a fleeting moment. We were utterly surprised but we should not have been. Both of the girls shrieked with joy. 'Oh Percy,' yelled Judy, 'I knew you would come.'

Bob smiled with delight and said, 'He always makes his best jump when he comes to greet you. You've always got to have your cameras at the ready.' Mine were still in my waterproof bag.

Percy was obviously in a joyful mood and he stayed with us before going back to the fishing boat. Next we saw him by the pot marker buoys. We ran backwards and forwards and chatted to the fishermen, waiting as always for the sudden appearance of a fin or a spectacular leap, never knowing when or where it would happen. Bob banged one of his diving fins on the side of the inflatable and Percy came upside down from beneath the boat to investigate. Sometimes the dolphin swam upside down alongside, showing us his white underbelly. At other times he would ride just in front of the bows with Judy shrieking with delight and saying, 'I've got him!' every time she clicked the shutter of her camera.

When I put on my mask and fins and slipped into the clear water Percy immediately came to see me, and we started to play a game of tag. He would keep just ahead, no matter how fast I swam, twisting and turning, and then suddenly vanishing from sight with a few thrusts of his tail. I would look up to Judy who would shriek his latest position to me. The tide was running quite fast, but I was too engrossed with our game to notice that we were being swept rapidly towards a dangerous rock where people were fishing from the land with rod and lines. I climbed back aboard and Bob took us back to the fishing buoy.

'The tide is running fast now,' he said. 'It's time for him to feed and I doubt if he'll come back with us.'

However, when we got to the fishing buoy Percy was already there. I leapt over the side again and was once more entranced by my proximity to the dolphin. The underwater visibility was good, and I could see his scars clearly. Tricia, who could not swim, wanted to jump overboard. She put her arm in the water, not caring that she was wearing her watch. Nothing seemed to matter to her except being close to the dolphin. Before long I was once again being carried back towards Godrevy by the tide. Eventually, unwillingly, I climbed back into the boat again.

Percy followed us part of the way back to Portreath, then made one final pass before leaving. The engine of the inflatable was not behaving quite as it should, but the boat's erratic movement did not matter. We were all filled with the joys of renewing our friendship with Percy. Tricia said she could see him much more clearly, and that he stayed much closer than when she had first met him at Godrevy lighthouse the previous year. She insisted he was even more friendly, and Bob confirmed that this was the most friendly he had ever been. Were we entering a new phase in his relationship with humans? The skies were still grey when we got back to Portreath, but the sun radiated from us.

There was a slight surf running up the beach, and Bob decided to take the boat in backwards with the bows pointing out towards the oncoming waves. We paddled the final few yards and I prepared to jump overboard to steady the boat in its final surge. Bob told the girls to stay aboard, but Tricia fell over and could hardly stand under the weight of her four soaked wool sweaters. Even so, she was shrieking with laughter as she clambered out of the surf.

'What about your watch?' asked Bob.

'Oh, bugger the watch. What does a watch matter compared with seeing Percy,' she said, still laughing.

A hot shower and a sad farewell preceded the long drive to London, but when I reached Bodmin Moor the sun broke through and flooded the countryside with soft evening light. Occasional banks of bluebells and the tender pink flowers of campion decorated the roadside and created blurred fleeting images on a voyage in which time had no relevance. I was on auto-pilot. In my mind I was still rushing through the sea on the inflatable with Percy swimming alongside.

The next news I had of Percy came directly from Portreath one week later. I was being treated to a special meal by my daughter Melanie, as a Father's Day present when the telephone rang. It was my son Ashley who had spent many joyful hours in the sea with Donald. Ashley told me that he had just been in the sea with Percy. He had found it a wonderful and exhilarating experience, with the dolphin leaping high over him. Ashley then relayed a message from Bob, who wanted me to know that Percy was getting more and more playful and friendly every day.

· 11 ·

Paradise Bay

Part of the launch of my book *The Magic of Dolphins* took the form of a film-show in London organised jointly by International Dolphin Watch and the World Wildlife Fund. One of the people who attended the presentation was Madelyn Freeman, a lady whose close affinity with the sea and its inhabitants was already known to me. I had first met her when she was living and working on a diving boat in the Red Sea. Using only fins, mask and snorkel, she had seemed to flow through the water like a seal, as if it was her natural element. Madelyn, a perceptive and sensitive person with a bubbling sense of humour and an infectious laugh, had studied psychic phenomena and was intrigued by the idea of a spiritual, extra-sensory connection between humans and dolphins. Her idea was given added weight when she read of my and Maura Mitchell's experiences with Donald the dolphin and saw the film I showed in London. When she heard about Percy and the Dolphin Link Project in Cornwall she decided to visit the West Country to experience for herself the dolphin magic, and to exchange views with James Wharram on some of the esoteric aspects of Polynesian culture. She also worked out how she was going to behave when she met Percy in the water.

I was not surprised, therefore, to receive a letter from her in which she described her first encounter with Percy, which took place on Tuesday, 19 June, 1984, on a flat calm day. Here is Madelyn's description of what happened when she adopted her own personalised approach to Percy – whom she referred to as she!

I began by finning down a good ten feet and turning over on my back while finning along horizontally – she was circling and sensing and began to respond to what I was doing. It was during this initial contact that I had the distinct impression she was looking through my mask more directly *into* my eyes. I had become 'objectively' aware of my 'self'. It's a subtle little manoeuvre; say you are at a cocktail party and someone begins to examine you more 'intently' and part of your 'self' (or divided 'attention') steps aside and 'sees' or senses the other's shift of attention towards you. And your self-awareness begins to heighten and you sense yourself through their eyes. She began to respond to my various sea movements. At one stage we were eyeball to eyeball, separated by about five feet, as she turned to face me head on, momentarily suspended. When I began to fin *hard* [having seen her in the Red Sea, I knew Madelyn could swim extremely fast] she took off like a BOLT!! and disappeared.

Madelyn stayed in the water, without a wetsuit, for about forty-five minutes. While she was taking a short breather, Percy made some spectacular leaps during which Madelyn felt the dolphin was looking directly into the boat. Madelyn's second immersion with Percy was shorter and she was eventually overtaken by the cold. Sea conditions then changed and she was not able to return to the sea during the course of the week.

In order to understand Percy's psyche I wanted to see the wild dolphin through as many different eyes and minds as possible. I was therefore pleased that a person like Madelyn, who I knew was sensitive and had spent hundreds of hours in the sea, should have an opportunity to swim with him, and asked her to send me a note of her feelings and observations. I was especially interested to discover why Madelyn considered that Percy was female.

Telling the sex of a dolphin is difficult. Size is one way of doing it as female Bottlenose dolphins are usually slightly

18 It was some canoists who first brought to my attention the presence of a friendly wild dolphin off the coast of Brittany.

19 Percy came up and examined me before pushing hard against my foot with his beak to propel me rapidly through the water.

20 Percy signalled his pleasure in body language when Laurie
Emberson abandoned his camera and went back into the sea just
to play.

21-3 Percy played vigorous games with me, but when Tricia got into the water he immediately became gentle.

smaller than the males. But, as with humans, there are many instances where males are smaller than females, and considerably greater differences can exist between sub-groups of the same species, as with different races of humans, e.g. the Zulus and Pygmies in Africa. The short-coming of using size as a sex guide was amply illustrated by Jean Louis, who was a female of about the same size as the definitely male Donald.

The quickest reliable way to tell the sex of an animal – examining the external reproductive appendages – is not normally possible with dolphins because Nature has so arranged the anatomy of dolphins that all the organs associated with reproduction are hidden away, thus pro-ducing the most streamlined shape possible. In the female the two mammary glands, which are close to the tail fluke, are concealed except when suckling. Two other slits, very near to one another, and also close to the tail, hide the urinary outlet and the anus. Thus the female has four openings, whereas the male has two separate slits, one for the penis and the other for the anus. All these openings close so securely that the slits are often barely visible in the smooth underside of the dolphin.

A feminist later pointed out, jokingly, that I was a typical male chauvinist to assume automatically that Percy was male – and I had to admit that the thought that this friendly wild dolphin might be a female had not entered my head. At the time of my first fleeting encounters I was too caught up with the thrill of meeting the dolphin in the sea to concern myself with his or her sex. Despite our subsequent encoun-ters I had not been able to study Percy's underside in sufficient detail to make absolutely sure that he was male because he was always moving so fast. However, later events were to reveal beyond all doubt that Percy was male.

I made my next visit to Cornwall on 1 July, before receiving Madelyn's letter. After attending a Council Meeting of the British Sub-Aqua Club at the Underwater Centre at Fort Bovisand, I drove to Portreath, arriving very late at night and going straight to an upstairs apartment, where I found a welcome-note from Judy saying she did not expect to see me before 10 a.m. the next day.

However, my first contact with the outside world was well before that, since I was greeted when I woke by Bob's cheerful face peering in through the open bedroom window. He had climbed up on to the balcony, using a ladder, to inform me that a group from the Dolphin Link in Devoran had arrived and was preparing to set sail to meet Percy.

All plans for a leisurely launch into the day were abandoned, and after a hurried piece of toast and a cup of coffee I joined Bob on the beach. We cruised out to the *Tiki*, a 20-foot catamaran which nestled quietly on the water about 150 yards off-shore. Then, leaving the catamaran to sail behind us in the breeze which was springing up, we set off in Bob's inflatable to make first contact with Percy.

Conditions were perfect and Percy came bounding over to us well before we reached Godrevy Island. As usual the air was electric when Percy was around, with the two female passengers shrieking with delight and talking to the dolphin. The water was very clear, and after first contact we decided to see how he would react to the yellow aquaplane being trailed behind the boat. Since Percy obviously enjoyed the experience, I jumped overboard for an easy ride through the water. I was aware of Percy's presence but could see him only if he came somewhat ahead of me. I wished I had his wide vision.

After my spell in the water with Percy we were surprised to see the blue sails of the catamaran making good progress towards us. The dolphin took off and joined the catamaran as soon as it came within about 200 yards. It was accompanied by the orange Humber inflatable we had used in France. With two inflatables and the catamaran Percy had a choice of three boats to play with. He obviously enjoyed the catamaran immensely, much to the delight of everyone aboard – which included James and Hanneke. There are strong currents in the dangerous waters along the north coast of Cornwall, and sailing a catamaran calls for con-

stant vigilance. So James and Hanneke had to tack frequently to stay in the same area – especially because of the
speed with which they were skimming across the sea. The
red hulls of the catamaran looked beautiful as they sliced
through the deep blue water, and white foam frothed up
from the leading edges of the bows.

Bob suggested that we went into a nearby bay, one of
Percy's favourite spots. I was making up my own names
for different parts of the coastline, and as the result of
subsequent events I decided to call this place Paradise
Bay.

We dropped anchor about 200 yards off-shore. I could
see the rope stretching down to the sandy bottom about
15 feet below us. A short time later the catamaran came
skimming in with the inflatable alongside, and the dolphin
alongside too. The sails were quickly hauled down and the
three boats were anchored together in the tranquil bay with
the dolphin swimming around.

I expected Percy to swim off after a short time, but he did
not. Even when his friendly fishing boats came past he
ignored them completely and stayed with us throughout
our stay. I had already made contact with him (not physical
contact) by gliding along on the aquaplane. When the first
snorkeller went in from the catamaran Percy went up close
to him, swimming around curiously and then zooming
down to the sea bed to inspect the anchor before coming
back to the snorkeller floating on the surface.

There then followed an astounding number of incidents
during which Percy came closer and closer to the humans.
He behaved differently with each diver. When André went
into the water Percy was very gentle. André was not a
strong swimmer and was wearing a wetsuit. He lay on the
surface of the sea and Percy came up and pushed his beak
against him, gently shoving the floating snorkeller through
the water. The next person to go in was a strong swimmer,
and Percy became very boisterous, leaping around, much to
everyone's delight. Then a young man from the shore swam
out and started to dive around us. He was wearing fins, but

no mask. He was a powerful swimmer and I could see his white body moving swiftly and confidently through the clear water. Percy took an immediate liking to this nearly naked skindiver and swam round him. It was a touching and beautiful sight – the green, weed-covered rock set on the yellow sand, with a white-bodied human swimming through the clear water and a grey dolphin gliding effortlessly, but curiously, around.

Throughout the day the sun shone down from a cloudless sky. We enjoyed the coffee and biscuits Judy had prepared, and all spent some time on the catamaran, making occasional visits to shore. There were just a few people on the beach and several swam out into the bay to join us. The fresh green foliage on the cliff-tops, the brown rocks and the deep blue sea provided a perfect backdrop for this fairystory of interspecies harmony.

At the end of the afternoon we reluctantly moved out of the bay. There was little wind and the catamaran could not sail easily back to Portreath against the current. After a few trial runs the orange inflatable was lashed to one of the hulls to act as a tug-boat. We were all surprised at the ease with which it propelled the catamaran through the water. Percy loved the new game, and swam between the hulls, ahead and astern, as well as circling the novel floating machine. He did not follow us all the way back to Portreath, but peeled off with the one final leap we had learned to recognise as his farewell gesture.

We sped ahead and soon had the inflatable beached. Within a short space of time the boat was unloaded and we were sitting down on the grassy terrace outside Beach House enjoying a welcome cup of tea and freshly baked scones topped with home-made strawberry jam and Cornish cream. As we sat enjoying ourselves, we saw the red hulls of the *Tiki* appear round Gull Rock, and within a short time the catamaran was anchored in the bay. The gear was soon stowed and the catamaran was brought ashore. After hauling the *Tiki* well up the beach the Dolphin Link crew departed for Devoran.

I stayed at Beach House and we made plans for an evening out. Before we left, however, I had one more delightful surprise to come. In a telephone conversation with my daughter Melanie, I was told that she was drinking champagne to celebrate the fact that she was pregnant. One of the other guests, who had recently become a grandmother, was delighted for me and expounded the joys of being a grandparent. I was able to confirm her predictions after my grand-daughter Rebecca was born, on 22 February, 1985.

We had a lot to celebrate and that evening enjoyed a superb meal at the Trebarrack Cottage Restaurant at Rosudgeon. To round off the evening we drove down to Prussian Cove to look at the sea by the light of a tiny new moon.

The next day I had, reluctantly, to leave Portreath in order to give a lecture at the Duchy Grammar School at Carnon Down. The sea conditions were good and the crew from Devoran was coming across to go out and see Percy again. None the less, I honoured my commitment and was rewarded by a very enjoyable and successful affair, terminated with a school dinner of sweet-and-sour sausage, followed by jam sponge and lumpy custard.

On the hurried drive back to Portreath I was aware that the wind had got up, and when I arrived at Smugglers' Cove I was informed by Bob that the crew from Devoran had been unable to make contact with Percy on their first run towards Godrevy. In view of the deteriorating weather they had decided to abandon the search and had brought the catamaran back into the safety of the bay. Having rushed back, I was very sorry not to be able to go out and see Percy.

'If you can't see him from the water – how about watching him from the land?' suggested Bob.

With Butch, the dog, in the back, we set off in the Volvo along the coast towards Godrevy to hunt for Percy. We looked over the cliffs at a couple of his favourite spots without success, then sat down opposite Godrevy looking at the smooth water in the lee of the island and the very choppy water adjoining it. Bob's eagle eye spotted a black fin rise briefly at the interface.

'He's feeding,' said Bob as he pointed out the place where the dolphin had just surfaced. From our vantage point in the sun, but out of the chilling wind, we spent a pleasant hour watching Percy while Bob told us of the video-recording that Christina Lockyer had made from the same spot.

That evening Bob fired up his barbecue, and we had an enjoyable meal on the lawn overlooking the sea before departing for Devoran where I was scheduled to give another film-show. We all crowded into the hot, blacked-out attic. Before my movie of Donald I showed a film of a friendly wild dolphin named Opo who visited a small fishing village called Opononi in New Zealand in 1955. With the behaviour of Percy still very fresh in our minds we were able to compare the antics of all three friendly wild dolphins.

We were sad that Ruth had not joined the crew on the catamaran during the magic day, since somebody had had to stay back at base and look after the place, so we agreed that if conditions were good the next day Bob and I would take her out with us in the inflatable to see Percy. English weather is notoriously capricious. As the following day was to be the last of my visit I was hoping hard that the weather god would look favourably on the requests I beamed in his direction.

He did. The next day was perfect, with little wind. But before I could go out Percy-hunting I had yet another lecture engagement, this time at the County Primary School in Devoran. I love giving film-shows, but once again I must admit that I did not like leaving Portreath with a flat-calm sea, knowing that by the time I returned at midday the weather could have deteriorated and I would have to leave without saying farewell to Percy. However, as it turned out, the gods were smiling on me.

The films were well received by the children, who shrieked with delight when they saw Opo and Donald tossing balls into the air. I collected Ruth from the Dolphin Link Centre and headed towards Portreath. A phone call to Bob had already established that we were in a 'GO' situation, and when we arrived he was already at sea in his inflatable, waiting for us. Judy hastily shoved the lunch she had prepared between some slices of bread and we joined Bob aboard his Zodiac inflatable for another dolphin contact . . . as always hoping that Percy would be willing to make it.

There was a short chop, and the inflatable bumped across the waves. The sun glinted off the wave-crests giving the sea the appearance of a piece of deep blue Lurex cloth stretching to the horizon.

There were many buoys in the water, indicating the presence of crab pots, but no fishing boats, since it was low water and the boats could not get in and out of the harbours. We were not greeted by Percy when we motored past Paradise Bay so we headed on to Godrevy Island, where we had seen him on the previous day. Again, we were granted no sighting. After circling the island completely, we headed back.

'Perhaps he's in the cove where we saw him yesterday,' said Bob, as we headed off in that direction.

And sure enough, when we got to the headland adjacent to the cove, there was Percy waiting for us. He immediately swam up to the inflatable and we could see him riding the bow wave through the clear water. Then he switched his attention to the stern and rode the V-shaped wake that ran behind the boat.

We lured him into Paradise Bay and threw over the anchor. I slipped into the water and once again felt the magical joy of swimming with a wild dolphin. Ruth was also in the water, and the two of us frolicked with Percy. After noticing the boat moving off a couple of times I discovered this was due not to Bob, but to Percy. The dolphin would dive down, pick up the anchor and, with the chain draped across his head, move it a few paces before dropping it back on the sand. When I came up and told Bob he replied, 'He's moving us away from the rocks,' implying that this was just what you would expect an intelligent friendly dolphin to do under the circumstances.

Percy was in a playful mood. A swimmer came out from the beach wearing a drysuit and I expected Percy to move off to say hello to him. But he didn't. The newcomer made a lot of noise and snorted into the water, presumably to attract the dolphin's attention. But Percy ignored him completely. He seemed an uncouth fellow. When I started to feel cold I climbed reluctantly back into the boat and we headed towards the shore and beached on the sand. We had our lunch and let the sun warm us through. Several people swam out into the bay, including the noisy person who continued to make his presence audibly felt, but Percy had gone. After lunch we left the idyllic beach and Bob suggested that we should try to pick up Percy and lure him to the lee of the Godrevy lighthouse, where it would be slack water and we would find another calm place. Percy joined us shortly after we turned the headland and escorted us to the desired location.

I peered over the side of the boat and could see the kelp under the sea very clearly. The water was exceptionally clear since the tide had not started to run. When it did, a stream of brown-red water would run through the channel between Godrevy Island and the mainland.

Ruth got into the water first, and lay still while Percy pushed her about. When she was vigorous he started to jump around her. I joined them in the water and looked down into the underwater forest. When we had seen Percy from the shore the day before he had looked jet black. Today, he was pale grey, and the sun reflected from the waves above him provided a constantly changing pattern of dancing light over his body.

I spent two hours in the water with Percy. During that time he allowed progressively more and more physical contact. I was able to stroke him when he swam past, and once again felt the delicious touch of the hard yet soft, smooth yet not slimy texture of a dolphin's skin. If I lay still in the water with my feet extended Percy would come up and nose them gently. When I held my hands slowly towards him he would come and look intently in my face. A slight movement of my hands, however, would send him away in a trice. He would twist vigorously in the water and rush away as if to say, 'You can't catch me.' It was like a child developing spontaneously a game of tag.

I then started to let Percy come up to my fins, and we both discovered that he could push me along by putting his beak against the ball of my foot. On one occasion he pushed me vigorously towards the lighthouse for 50 yards. The game continued to develop until he would come up beneath me, when I was vertical in the water, and let me put my fin on the tip of his beak, whereupon I pushed as hard as I possibly could and launched myself away from him. He obviously relished this game, repeatedly coming up beneath me, pushing me out of the water so that I was almost standing on his head ... with three-quarters of my body out of the water. It was a show of complete trust on his part, a major breakthrough. I was in positive contact with a wild dolphin and both of us were pushing hard against one another with almost the physical intimacy of a friendly wrestling contest.

Now I had a good chance to look closely at Percy's belly, and I could make sure of the dolphin's sex. After having been visited by Madelyn, James Wharram had started calling the dolphin Priscilla. When the possibility of Percy's being female had first been put to me I had had to admit that I could not be 100 per cent certain that Percy was not Priscilla. Now I could. So I laughingly told Ruth that I knew James liked being surrounded by females – but Percy was most definitely male.

Despite having been in the water for such a long time I was not cold at all, and I was sad when Bob said that as he and Judy were going out that night it was time to head back for Portreath.

Bob knew Percy's habits well and predicted what he would do next, so we skimmed along the line joining the rough water with the smooth and waited for the dolphin to leap up alongside. Which he did – not exactly according to Bob's predictions, but then Percy did have to show us that he was still master of the situation.

Percy stayed with us for a while but decided not to escort us all the way back to Portreath. There was still not a cloud in the sky. We diverted briefly to have a look at a seal, and we passed Ralph's Cupboard, which was cast in shadow. I saw the golden strand of the beach at the end of the cutting through the cliff wall. Then we were passing Gull Rock and skimming across the sparkling blue water into the bay at Portreath. A feeling of joy filled us all.

I gave Ruth a lift back to the Dolphin Link Centre in my car before starting off on the long journey north. When I left Devoran the sun was still high but its power was waning. The air was filled with a soft yellow light that cast the curves of the countryside into gentle relief. The miles of the long journey sped by, leaving me unaffected. I felt more like a spirit than a solid human being. It was as if my very bones were made of joy.

During my various contacts with Percy a new term had come into common use, particularly by people associated with the media. It was 'mind-blowing', and it kept going through my brain on the homeward journey. If I had been asked at the time to define the term I would have done so as follows: 'The feeling experienced after meeting a friendly wild dolphin in the sea and having a really positive inter-action with him.'

· 12 ·

Percy Exposes Himself

Media interest is contagious. Once one reporter picks up a topic the editor considers newsworthy, then that same subject is likely to be covered by the competition. In the case of Percy the newsmen started to create their own news because they became personally involved in the story. A typical example was Francesca Hanikova's report in the *Camborne-Redruth Packet* of 8 August, 1984, with the headline, blazened across the centre-page spread: 'THE DAY I CAME FACE-TO-FACE WITH PERCY OF PORTREATH'.

> Saturday, 5 August 1984, will always stand out in my memory as the day of a once-in-a-lifetime experience – the day I swam with a dolphin.
>
> It was one of those chances a reporter dreams about, when a run-of-the-mill story throws up something really special.
>
> For me, the result of a story about the sighting of a dolphin was an invitation to meet him face-to-face – all 14 feet of him.
>
> Percy of Portreath was discovered by Bob Holborn three years ago, and during that time their relationship has developed into something very special – a man and a dolphin sharing mutual trust and love.

The article was illustrated with large, excellent pictures taken by Phil Lockley, and the narrative went on to describe the coming together of the reporter, the photographer, Sue Jago and Bob in the sea with Percy. Percy put on an excellent show that terminated as follows:

He took off to at least eight feet into the air and seemingly remained poised in an elegant arc before dipping into the water with hardly a splash.

Francesca also commented on the profound effect Percy was having on the Holborn household:

Bob and Judy, whose luxury home overlooks Smugglers Cove at Portreath, are also very proud of their dolphin friend, around which much of their life revolves.

Instead of baby albums visitors are treated to Percy albums, and among Bob's video collection, one of Percy usurps James Bond in the ratings.

And if you think interest in Percy borders on obsession, Judy would agree. She has to wash up dishes in the bathroom because Bob – who runs holiday chalets in Portreath – never seems to have time to complete the kitchen in their home.

But like everyone else, Judy's heart has been won over. Mine certainly has, and I'm already looking forward to my next meeting with Percy.

During August and September, Bob found himself the focus of much media attention. He never tired of talking about Percy and was always willing to take those with an interest out to see his dolphin. He openly admitted that he loved Percy. He became the dolphin's self-appointed guardian and threatened severe retribution on anyone he considered might threaten Percy in any way. Bob was an extremely strong, and occasionally a volatile, character, so Percy could not have had a more powerful minder. However, in addition to being protective towards Percy, he was concerned that the dolphin should be portrayed in a way that would not offend anyone, and in this respect a new aspect of Percy's behaviour became something of an embarrassment to him. It was referred to in Francesca's report as follows:

He's quite a frisky fellow too, mind you, and he took

quite a fancy to barmaid Sue – a local surf life-saver –
who had to shake off his amorous intentions.

Francesca was delicately referring to the fact that Percy
had exposed his penis, rubbing it against Sue. Although it
was of no consequence to him, Bob was concerned that
some of the visitors he took out to see Percy might find such
behaviour distasteful, and that it might frighten small
children. He therefore told Percy not to be 'fruity' and tried
to correct the dolphin in the same way he would have
attempted to control a dog who behaved in a similar
manner.

It was a situation I had been through many times before,
because Donald had behaved in a similar way. The fact that
I had to remove the section of my film in which Donald
showed his penis before I was allowed to show it to huge
audiences at the National Geographic Society in Wash-
ington, DC, supported the view that such scenes were
unacceptable to the general American public, who expected
to see dolphins portrayed as cuddly wholesome, playful
and friendly fellow creatures. I agreed that dolphins can
indeed have these attributes, but was anxious that we
should not over-sentimentalise them or reduce them to
sterile, bland, lovable cartoon characters. I felt we should
accept the fact that they have guts and kidneys. They
defecate, urinate and also copulate.

A dolphin's penis is composed mainly of fibro-elastic
tissues and can be exposed and retracted at will. It is
probably the most tactile-sensitive and vulnerable part of
his anatomy, and it is usually kept well protected inside the
abdominal wall. It will be exposed only in situations where
the dolphin feels secure.

To me, the exposure of Percy's penis was therefore a
display of trust, and as such represented another major step
forward in the breakdown of the barriers between humans
and dolphins. Having so openly displayed his trust, Percy
was not inhibited by the codes of conduct imposed by
sexually-repressive Westernised societies. He rubbed his

penis indiscriminately against those he trusted, regardless of their sex. He was surely intelligent enough not to be attempting to mate with them. So why did he do it?

Dolphins are sensitive and sensuous creatures. Occasionally Percy masturbated. However, because of the frequency and manner in which he used his penis I think these were acts not of repetitious masturbation, but of sensual pleasure, with sexual overtones. I suspect Jean Louis may have been engaging in the female equivalent of the same experience when she swam up and down rubbing her abdomen against the ropes of moored boats, which I watched her do frequently.

During the learning processes of early human life, the young child first looks at a new object, then touches it, and then puts it into his or her mouth. Dolphins do not have fingers and lips to fulfil these exploratory investigations. But they do have highly evolved brains and inquisitive minds. It is thus not unreasonable to propose that Percy increased his awareness and appreciation of the humans he came into contact with by stroking them with his penis. Exposure of his penis was not the gesture of perverted promiscuity that many people considered it to be. My interpretation was that it was an act of trust that added to his overall appreciation of the humans upon whom he bestowed the privilege of close physical contact. When he rubbed himself against Tricia Kirkman at a later stage she compared the act with her own appreciation of a flower. To her, touch was extremely important. She said, 'I can look at a flower, I can smell a flower, but to understand the full beauty of a flower I must also *touch* it.'

I experienced for myself this new turn in Percy's behaviour when I returned to Portreath on 28 July, 1984. During the next couple of days I swam and dived with Percy and noticed several aspects of his behaviour which indicated that he was progressively developing a closer relationship with humans. Sometimes he would lie just below the surface, belly uppermost, and virtually offer his flippers to a snorkeller, who would be towed along if he took hold of them. The tow was sometimes accompanied by a display of the penis, which he allowed humans to touch with their hands.

I felt it was almost as if Percy had discovered a new sense and was trying it out on everything. After diving with him in Paradise Bay, a clinker-built boat with children aboard came past, and Percy took off in hot pursuit. So did we, and the two boats headed towards Portreath side by side. The children were entranced by the dolphin, who often swam between Bob's inflatable and their boat.

I saw a pair of tiny hands appear on the gunwale and then a very young face appeared over the side of the boat. It broke into a beautiful smile as Percy surfaced alongside and swam on the surface, keeping pace with the boat and looking at the child who was watching him. We were progressing at about five knots when Percy went under the other boat, turned upside down and rubbed his penis against the keel while swimming at the same speed as the boat. This was not visible to those aboard, of course. But I could see his tail fluke pumping up and down just a few feet away from the whizzing propeller which could have inflicted severe injury.

This behaviour demonstrated Percy's complete mastery of his element. To those on the inflatable it appeared to be an act of recklessness, and we were concerned for his safety. But it could just as well have been an act of sheer bravado on the part of an adolescent dolphin who, although apparently fully grown, had just reached sexual maturity.

I discussed the subject of Percy's apparent promiscuity with James Wharram, who had been recording Percy's behaviour in detail, using a tape-recorder on site, to provide material for later scientific analysis. James mentioned that the members of some tribes spend a lot of time rubbing noses, which is equivalent to Westernised people kissing. This he maintained was a gesture of sensory enjoyment which was not necessarily related to sexual activity, although it could be. He regarded the exposure of Percy's penis as a quite spontaneous, uninhibited gesture which we should not attempt to suppress. He mentioned the hypercri-tical, sexually suppressive society in which we lived, and said that in many so-called primitive human cultures, Percy's behaviour would be regarded as quite natural and certainly not embarrassing. My own feeling was that such people would probably find the exposing of Percy's penis just like so much of his other behaviour, entertaining and amusing.

I have discussed this issue, as well as the whole subject of human-dolphin relations, with many people, among them a New Zealander, Wade Doak, who suggested that when attempting to understand the psyche of dolphins we could approach the subject as if we were trying to understand their nearest human equivalents. These, he suggested, were the nomadic aboriginal Australians before they came under the influence of Western civilisation. I found this an extremely rewarding concept to consider. Although the aborigines fabricated a few weapons, they were not tool-makers in the Western sense. Their values were not there-fore based on possessions – which is how the great majority of Western people judge their fellow men. If an aborigine had made a table and chair and attempted to carry them with him on his walkabouts, they would be impediments, not assets. Far more important to these people were the spirits that lived in the rocks.

The aborigines did not attempt to dominate nature by planting crops or building permanent houses. Their way of life was based upon being very close to nature and living in harmony with it. Survival depended upon being exquisitely sensitive to natural forces, and flowing with them. They wore no clothes. Unfortunately it was a way of life that was little documented before it was destroyed. The ethos of the dolphins seems to fit more comfortably with a stone-age culture based upon the dream time than it does with present-day civilisations based upon control and power.

A few aborigines who have adapted to the computer age are now trying bravely to rediscover the lost culture and traditions of their forebears. If they can bridge that chasm, then there is a chance that we can span the even greater gap between humans and dolphins.

I had to accept the fact that it was difficult to be totally objective in assessing why Percy exposed his penis, and that most people who saw it happen briefly, perhaps in a short clip of film, would inevitably make a judgment based upon their own libido, sexual morality and inhibitions. Comments ranging from, 'He's a randy old bugger', to 'He's holding out the finger of friendship', were immediate responses by two different men. Such comments reflect the diversity of opinions on the subject, and also the dangers of being anthropomorphic.

To the majority of people, however, the exposure of Percy's penis was a source of amusement which they regarded in much the same way as they did saucy seaside postcards. In view of the air of happiness and frivolity that accompanied Percy most of the time, this was not a bad thing. Not everyone had to be as analytical as I was. It was far more important that they should enjoy touching Percy and being touched by him. If they went away with the attitude that he was a saucy dolphin, did it really matter?

· 13 ·

Percy Becomes Assertive

As a result of Percy's antics off the coast of Cornwall I was invited to do the morning phone-in programme, BBC Radio 4's *Tuesday Call*, on Tuesday, 7 August, 1984. I spent the evening before the show very pleasantly with the programme's producer, Kay Evans, and her husband. To make sure I wasn't delayed or missing, the next-day accommodation was arranged for me in a hotel almost next door to Broadcasting House, in Langham Place.

During the programme itself Kay Evans monitored the calls coming in and selected which ones were passed to Sue McGregor, who was with me in the adjoining studio. Sue did a masterly job, gently manoeuvring the callers and myself, balancing my reply with the question and then moving smoothly on to the next topic. For fifty minutes I discussed with doctors, housewives and children as diverse a range of aspects relating directly and indirectly to the life of dolphins as can be imagined. The programme had the excitement of a live, unscripted show, unpredictable because it depended upon the listening audience to provide the questions. Everyone was delighted with the outcome. As we packed into the lift afterwards one of the other passengers commented, 'You lot seem to be very happy.' 'Yes,' replied Sue. 'We've just done a super programme and we are all still on a high.'

It certainly was a wonderful feeling, and I floated over the London pavements towards my car which was parked near by. Six hours later, still feeling elated, I drove into the car park at Beach House in Portreath.

Beach House was becoming a focal point for those with an active interest in dolphins, with people from different countries and backgrounds converging there. When I arrived a group from Sweden was camped near by. They had read my books and were setting up a centre for the study of whales and dolphins in Sweden very broadly based upon the lines of International Dolphin Watch.

It was a fascinating and diverse group. The eldest was a charming professorial gentleman, whose eyes sparkled as he expounded his views on the metaphysical subjects related to dolphins and whose delightful, sometimes fanciful, theories were sprinkled with wit and humour. His male colleague was Lasse Löfgren, who had just published an impressive and colourful tome entitled *Ocean Birds*, the outcome of over ten years studying and photographing birds at sea. During his world-wide travels as a merchant marine officer Lasse had also become fascinated by the large marine mammals, and these were becoming his major interest, and the subject for his next book. The other two members of the group were younger. One was a Swedish girl with blonde hair. The other was an attractive dark-haired American girl who worked in Sweden. They all spoke impeccable English.

When we debated the possibility of dolphins and humans cooperating together, Lasse informed me of a unique situation where this already happened off the coast of Brazil. He told me that he had seen fishermen standing at the edge of the sea waiting for dolphins to bring the fish towards the shore. The dolphins would herd the fish into a ball and then work them towards the fishermen, like sheepdogs. When the fish were just a few feet away from them the fishermen would cast their hand-thrown nets out over the water. The weighted rim of the circular net would sink through the water faster than the centre where the fish were trapped. It was a practice that had been going on for many decades and always involved the same dolphins. From interviews he had with the older fishermen Lasse discovered that the life-span in the wild of a Bottlenose dolphin, which is generally accepted to be about thirty years, may be considerably longer. This he derived from the fact that at least one dolphin, which could be precisely identified, had been helping the older fishermen in the same way for much longer than three decades. The fishermen had names for the helpful dolphins and knew when a new youngster appeared.

For me it was a fascinating example of atypical dolphin behaviour, and very relevant to our understanding of Percy. Most of the dolphins off the coast of Brazil behaved in a different way. They would herd the fish into balls and then charge into the concentrated food supply. This hunting/ feeding behaviour took place off-shore – well out of the range of hand-thrown nets. So why should a few dolphins repeatedly herd fish very close in-shore, knowing they would lose them to the fishermen?

Was it a truly altruistic gesture on the part of thinking dolphins towards fellow earth creatures who were obviously far less capable of procuring the same food for themselves? I had heard of situations in other parts of the world where humans had taken advantage of the practice of dolphins driving fish in-shore to take some of the feast for themselves. This happened, for instance, off the coast of Mauritania where the Imragen tribesmen wait for the dolphins to appear before setting their nets. The hunt is such a furious affair that many of the teeming mullet leap into the air to escape from the jaws of the marauding dolphins. The terrified fish also rush headlong into the nets of the fishermen, who wade out to take a harvest from the sea that would not be possible without the dolphins' help.

A somewhat similar situation exists in India. When dolphins coming through the estuary entrance into Chulka Lake are spotted, the native fishermen race down the beach carrying nets. Often with small boys assisting by holding one end of the net, the adults run through the shallows scooping up the fish that have been shepherded by the on-rushing dolphins. The dolphins mingle with the fishermen in a frenzy of fishing activity.

When two members of International Dolphin Watch, who had witnessed this happy collaboration between fishermen and dolphins, questioned one of those involved, the reply was, 'The dolphins are our friends. They show us when the fish are coming and bring them to us.'

I was keen to win Percy's cooperation with one of my experiments, but was unable to do so on 8 August because Bob had a full boat-load of passengers, which included the Swedish group. We bumped over a choppy sea to Paradise Bay, where Percy came bounding to meet us. After shooting a roll of pictures from the surface Lasse went into the water for a swim with Percy and to take underwater pictures with his Nikonos camera.

Then, to my surprise, the old gentleman quickly stripped off and went into the sea. The shock of the cold water caused him to make the most extraordinary grimaces, but when Percy approached and hooked his penis into the crook of the man's bare leg his expressions became even more extraordinary – much to the amusement of everyone aboard. Despite his surprise as Percy rubbed hard against him, he said he still felt it was an exploratory gesture on the part of the dolphin.

Then the two girls, dressed only in swimming costumes, got into the water. When Percy went to 'investigate' the Swedish girl she shrieked and swam to the side of the inflatable where she clung to one of the ropes. The reality of suddenly finding herself in the open sea, in such intimate contact with a powerful animal twice her length and four times her weight, was a big shock. She recovered her composure when Percy decided to give Lasse the benefit of his attention.

When we reviewed Percy's behaviour later the Swedish group, without exception, viewed the exposure of Percy's penis as a gesture of vulnerability.

I accepted this point of view, but I also saw it as a sign of Percy's growing self-assurance in the presence of humans. His increasing assertiveness was also demonstrated very clearly in several ways when I next went out to see him two days later. I still wanted to see if I could get a wild dolphin to cooperate voluntarily in a mechanical task. Bob and I therefore set out to find Percy and he followed us into a quiet cove where I lowered a newly-made Dobbsophone to the sea bed.

It consisted of a number of wine bottles tied with lengths of string to the stock of an old anchor, like the one I had used in France with Jean Louis. Percy watched with interest while I partially filled the bottles with air. When he came and knocked one of the bottles with his beak, so that it clanged against another, I really thought I was going to get his full cooperation and moved back in the hope that he would develop his discovery. But he didn't. I therefore moved in close again, knelt beside my apparatus, and gonged away. At this point, Percy swam behind me and very forcefully pinned me to the sea bed by pushing against the back of my knees with his beak. In the mean time, Bob swam away, found a spider crab and showed it to Percy, who took no interest in it whatsoever. Bob let it go and watched it scamper back to the safety of a crevice in the rocks. When the dolphin eventually decided to release me I felt it was time to conclude the experiment. With Bob's assistance the anchor was hauled back into the inflatable.

Having decided that the time for serious science was over I quickly jettisoned my aqualung and started to play with Percy on the surface. We engaged in a rumbustious game with Percy towing me through the water and careering around me at great speed – his wash rocking the inflatable.

We were fairly close in-shore and an adult couple swam out to see us. The lady was topless and when Percy approached her she shrieked. Then, to our utmost surprise, Percy butted her in the midriff and pushed her under the water. She came up choking. Bob offered assistance but she declined. She and her companion were both strong swimmers and immediately swam back to the beach.

I had already noticed that Percy had distinct preferences regarding people in the water and that he would completely ignore some swimmers, no matter how hard they tried to impose their company upon him. However, I had never seen him express his apparent disapproval of anyone so forcefully before.

Apart from a boat handler the only other passenger in the boat with us that day was Tricia Kirkman. She had acquired a wetsuit and was trying to pluck up courage to go into the water with Percy – despite the fact that she could not swim. When she saw what happened to the topless woman, who was obviously an extremely good swimmer, Tricia had to summon up every ounce of her courage to venture into the sea. I told her if she was quiet and gentle she would be all right.

She put on fins, mask and snorkel and slid very quietly over the side. Percy approached her and then turned upside down. Tricia grasped his fins as if they were outstretched arms. The dolphin very slowly towed her through the water. I quickly put a new film in my underwater camera, and when I got back into the sea Tricia, who had been alone in the water with the dolphin, was about seven yards from the boat. As I swam towards them I saw one of those sights that burnt into my memory and left a permanent image. Tricia was floating on the surface with her arms straight down and her hands resting very lightly on Percy's head. The dolphin was swimming very slowly forwards so that the two of them were gliding through the water. The red colour of Tricia's wetsuit reflected from the surface of the water contrasted with her long black flowing hair. It was a picture of great beauty, peace and harmony, one of those incidents in life which last only briefly, yet are extremely significant. Here was a woman who could not swim floating across the deep sea, propelled by a wild dolphin.

During her entire stay in the water Percy never gave Tricia one moment's cause for alarm. When she was eventually hauled back into the Zodiac she sat on one of the tubes with her legs dangling in the water. As she did so Percy slid up from the depths, raised his head out of the water and rested it on Tricia's lap. She bent her head down and Percy rose higher to gently touch her face with the tip of his beak.

In 1974 I saw my son ride on a wild dolphin. In 1984 I saw a wild dolphin kiss a lady.

Percy followed us back to Portreath, where Bob had other dolphin-watchers waiting for a trip. When we arrived off the beach Bob put down his anchor and left it on the sea bed with a rope attached to a marker buoy. As he ferried us ashore Bob said that was the sign he left for Percy to indicate he would be coming back shortly.

I did not wait to see if Percy stayed as I had an engagement with a film producer, David Pritchard, at the BBC studios in Plymouth. Knowing that Percy could disappear at any time I was anxious that the dolphin's rapidly growing friendship with humans should be recorded on film and be enjoyed by the millions who were less fortunate than myself and Bob.

Our meeting was extremely cordial. David explained that he was not in a position to produce a crew and the very considerable funding necessary for such a film just at the drop of a hat. He did say, however, that he had already commissioned a film about sea life in Cornwall and that we might be able to incorporate Percy's story into it. The man shooting the film was a freelance director/cameraman, Laurie Emberson. At that point Laurie arrived in David's office. After consuming several gin and tonics, during which I outlined Percy's story and the situation in Portreath, we all headed for the canteen.

Laurie was a very sensitive man, and the more I discussed dolphins with him the more I became convinced he would be an ideal choice to cover Percy's remarkable story on film. After a generous helping of best BBC treacle pudding and custard I left for home, looking forward to returning to Portreath after the weekend.

· 14 ·

Percy Rules

I enjoyed working with Laurie Emberson, who proposed that his film should explore the dolphin's view of the undersea world off the Cornish coast. The dolphin would look at us, instead of us looking at the dolphin. Laurie, an expert diver of long experience, was mentally well tuned to such an approach. He said he was keen to project the dignity of the animal we both knew and respected as the true master of the undersea world.

For two weeks the filming progressed despite the setbacks that invariably beset underwater movie-making. One grain of sand in the wrong place can cause major problems. Laurie handled his 16mm. cine-camera, which was encased in a waterproof pressure-resistant housing he designed and built himself, with meticulous care. Even so he had a minor leak which took a while to diagnose and cure. One of my underwater lights completely flooded. So quite a lot of time was spent dismantling and reassembling equipment.

I was not involved in all the filming sessions, and when we met on Friday, 17 August, Laurie told me that during a late afternoon session the previous day Percy's behaviour had become distinctly aggressive towards Bob. The dolphin biffed Bob very hard several times and ended by biting his hand with such force that he drew blood. At the time Bob was quite frightened, but when the three of us discussed the incident later, Bob said his pride was more hurt than his body. We were all seasoned divers and our collective diving experience was immense. Yet this incident made us sharply aware of just how little we knew about the immensely powerful animal we were proposing to go out and film.

In France Jean Louis had shown that dolphins do not always go to the aid of a drowning man. I knew of no incident in which a Bottlenose dolphin had attacked and seriously injured a human. Indeed, it was widely accepted that even when provoked dolphins do not retaliate aggressively. Could that myth be brought into question too?

Unlike sharks, whose teeth are razor sharp and designed to slice through flesh and bone, Percy had conical interlocking teeth devised to grasp prey. None the less, if he so desired, we had no doubt he could break our limbs like matchsticks. He could also dispatch us by ramming us with his beak, which is the time-honoured method reported to be used by dolphins for killing sharks. It was therefore with some concern that we set out to film him on the Friday morning.

It was another perfect day. There was hardly a breath of wind and the sea was flat calm. The above-water visibility was exceptional – every detail of the coastline could be seen with pinpoint sharpness. Bob commented that we could see Percy's entire territory. The Godrevy lighthouse, which often looks a long way from Portreath, appeared to be much closer. I retorted to Bob that depth under-water also appears to change with the visibility. Very clear water makes depths seem much less to the submerged diver.

We found Percy playing around a fishing boat. When the dolphin moved off with the fishing boat Bob dangled his folding anchor over the side. This tempted Percy back to us and he then followed our inflatable into Paradise Bay.

We had worked out a filming plan and it went like clockwork. I decided to wipe from my mind Bob's experience of the previous day, and went into the sea first. I told myself Percy would be his usual friendly self and I tried to project the thought to Percy. Whether he received it or not I do not know. He was not in the slightest bit aggressive or even assertive. He took little interest in the anchor but was absolutely fascinated by my powerful underwater light, which was cylindrical in shape. I held it with the beam pointing upwards for him to see. He looked at it intently and then put the tip of his beak right on the glass cover plate behind which the quartz iodine lamp glowed. All his movements were slow, deliberate and gentle, exactly what Laurie wanted for his film. When Laurie had exposed all his film I asked the under-water cameraman if he would pose for my still camera.

Percy obviously liked Laurie, whose graceful flowing movements indicated the man's natural affinity with the sea and its inhabitants. The visibility was good. The sun, reflected and refracted by the gently rippled surface of the sea, beamed into the depths. Patterns of light danced over the yellow sea bed, the dark green kelp fronds and Percy's smooth grey body.

Laurie's original idea was that his film would reflect a day in the life of a dolphin. Sequences taken at different times and places would be joined together to create this illusion. This posed problems of continuity, and I was reminded just how different the atmosphere can be in Cornwall from day to day, as well as from season to season, when we went for a meal one night to Carn Brea Castle. There was no moon. The sky was soot black. The Castle, which stood on the top of a pinnacle of high ground, was floodlit with yellow light. The swirling mists, blown by a gentle wind, gave it a mysterious eerie atmosphere. A film sequence taken that night would certainly not have conveyed a feeling of high summer.

Equal problems exist for the sub-aqua cameraman. Sunlight gives underwater sequences a special quality that brings them to life on film. Sometimes Laurie abandoned filming on dull days, even when sea conditions were good. He did so knowing that it would be difficult to edit any sequences taken into the sparkling shots filmed on sunny days.

All the film of the dolphin shot during August was mute.

David Pritchard arranged to take a full sound crew to Portreath on 3 September. I knew from previous experience that once summer was over the quality of the sea could change dramatically and irreversibly from a filming stand-point. Would the exceptionally good conditions we had up until August hold into September? A later event with another film crew in the same location made me appreciate in hindsight just what an extraordinary day Monday, 3 September, was.

I met Laurie Emberson, David Pritchard and the film crew from BBC Plymouth beside the harbour in Portreath at 9.30 a.m. We had a cup of coffee at a seafront café and discussed the plans for the shoot. The idea was that we would go to Godrevy and Laurie would film the boat arriving from sea level, thus representing the dolphin's view. I would be interviewed onboard and the dolphin would eavesdrop on the conversation before I got into the water with him. I and the crew would travel on a boat called *Calamar* which was skippered by Mark Law. Laurie and his assistant would work from their own dory. Bob would act as dolphin scout in his Zodiac.

The boats were loaded and we set out from the harbour at 10.30 a.m. At the last minute, at Bob's request, I transferred to his Zodiac as the sea was getting up. Seasickness can completely debilitate even the most willing sailor, and I wondered how the film crew would fare after the long haul in the fishing boat to Godrevy Island. However, I need not have worried. As soon as the convoy got into the bay Percy came to greet us. Plans were immediately changed. We would film in the bay at Portreath instead of going all the way to Godrevy.

I transferred to the fishing boat and the film crew were soon ready for me to do my interview sitting on the stern, with Bob in his inflatable just behind me. Percy stayed around us most of the time, occasionally moving off to frolic with a windsurfer who was skimming back and forth across the bay.

Eventually I rolled in backwards, filmed by Laurie who

was already in the water with his camera and recording my arrival in the sea from a dolphin's viewpoint. Bob joined me in the water. Percy enjoyed this turn of events. Having three divers in the water with him was more to his liking than just watching them fiddling around in their boats. However, his expectations were cut short when I was asked to return to the *Calamar* to continue my interview on the stern and Bob climbed back on to his inflatable. Setting up the sequence took a few minutes, by which time Bob had turned ashen and given his breakfast to the fishes. He decided to swim back to the shore, leaving us to look after his boat. I did my piece and then rolled backwards, dropping into the sea beside Laurie who was still trying to film from sea level. However, the sea had got progressively rougher and it was almost impossible for him to steady his camera. To add to the difficulties, Percy was nudging both of us all the time and generally causing havoc. Sometimes, just as he was about to take a shot, Laurie would be thumped in the back by the dolphin. Percy also kept nudging the underwater light I carried, which fascinated him.

Percy could easily swim through all the confusion, no matter how rough the water was. But Laurie was unable to emulate the dolphin's smooth motion with his camera running and could not get the footage he wanted.

It has become a tradition to do news reports for television at the scene of the action. Intrepid reporters in war zones duck from whizzing shells while still continuing to talk to the camera. In view of the lively circumstances in which we found ourselves, David Pritchard decided to do a news report on Percy in addition to providing material for Laurie's film. As a result, David asked me to stay in the water and do an interview, with him asking the questions from the boat.

However, with all the media attention he was receiving, Percy was fast becoming a prima donna. As I swam to the side of the *Calamar* and started to speak, the dolphin rushed up and started to push me away, as if to say, 'Hey, I'm supposed to be the star of this show.'

When I diverted my attention away from the cameras and towards Percy he responded immediately. I twirled in the water and he became more and more excited. Encouraged by me he reared out of the water and for a few seconds towered above me. I became completely caught up in a frenzy of excitement. I remember shouting in the general direction of the boat, 'I'd rather do this than have ten Rolls Royce cars!' – whereupon Percy leapt right out of the water and crashed back down again with an enormous splash, sending spray over everyone, and over the cameras. His wash added to the waves that were already rocking the boat. The sun shone down intermittently through the ragged grey and white clouds that were racing faster and faster across the sky.

After the protracted filming session we managed to get into the harbour, but not soon enough to moor up to the wall. The *Calamar* grounded in the middle of the harbour on the falling tide. So we ferried the passengers and their gear ashore using the inflatable, which had a very shallow draft.

After a quick refresher in the quayside pub we adjourned to Beach House. David Pritchard was delighted with the morning's work. The camera crew were also enthralled with what they had seen. Two of them had jumped into the sea with Percy during an intermission in the filming programme. By the time the crew left to return to Plymouth the sky was grey and rain was pelting down.

The same evening I went to Redruth railway station to pick up a would-be Percy watcher. The wind-blown rain, illuminated by the platform lights, looked like a studio effect as it swept down the track and peppered anxious sweethearts and huddled-up taxi drivers awaiting the arrival of the train. We were the only people to dine that night in a large restaurant near by. It was only 3 September, yet it seemed like winter. If the summer season really was over then we had made the final filming session by the skin of our teeth.

The West Country has been dubbed the English Riviera, I suspect by the Tourist Board. The climate certainly is often more clement in the south-west than in the north-east during the winter months. And it was in the hope that we would hit a mild spell that I agreed to attempt to find Percy for another television item, this time for a BBC children's programme entitled *Newsround Extra* which planned to deal with the controversial issue of dolphins in captivity, about which I have strong views. The idea was that I would be filmed in the sea with Percy and give my reasons why I thought dolphins should not be captured. My view would be opposed by a veterinary surgeon who would put his case for confinement.

As is usual with such programmes, arrangements were quickly made, and I telephoned Beach House several times to enlist Bob's cooperation. However, there was no reply, so I went ahead and chartered the *Calamar*. Tuesday, 30 October, was allocated for reconnaissance with an early start to catch the tide. When I arrived at the harbour I found Mark Law, the skipper, tossing crabpots up from the deck of his boat on to the quayside. The sea was rough and I walked to the harbour entrance to assess the situation. A stone pier projected out into the bay, forming a channel, with the cliffs opposite acting as the other wall. Waves sweeping into the bay moved down the man-made channel, getting weaker as they went, until they finally spent themselves in the harbour. Most of the time the channel was passable, but at unpredictable intervals a very large wave would ride into the harbour and set the boats dancing. We decided to wait until nine before attempting to make an exit.

We ran the gauntlet through the harbour entrance and into the bay. Just as we got clear a huge, proud wave towered towards us and threw itself on to the outermost end of the pier, sending white foam high into the air while the leading edge of the wave went hissing along the wall towards the unyielding shore. I was very glad we were able to ride out that freak wave in the relative safety of the open sea.

We revved the engine in the hope that Percy would be attracted by the sound, and circled in the bay. When he did not appear we headed towards Godrevy. However, we turned back for Portreath long before we got to the island, to avoid missing the tide and having to wait until the evening to get back to the harbour.

Although we had failed to find Percy I was hopeful that we would succeed the following day when we would have the film crew with us. If necessary we could stay out at sea all day long.

I arrived at the harbour at eight the next morning on Wednesday, 31 October. As I made my way to the *Calamar* I saw two fully kitted divers on the quayside who were not part of our group. I walked over to find out what they intended to do, and to my surprise I discovered they were two scientists I already knew, Christina Lockyer and Bob Morris. They told me they had a long-standing arrangement to go out with Bob – who turned up a few minutes later, looking very cheerful. He had arrived home from a holiday in Yorkshire the previous evening, which explained why I had been unable to make contact with him.

Bob launched his inflatable and headed out with the two divers aboard towards Godrevy Island. He agreed that he would find Percy and lure the dolphin to Fisherman's Cove, alias Paradise Bay, where we would join them later in the *Calamar*, a very much slower boat. Things seemed to be working out even better than I hoped.

I had enlisted the services of another friend, Terry Howard, to bring his small inflatable to Portreath for use as a scout boat. After being filmed leaving the harbour aboard the *Calamar* I transferred to Terry's boat to press ahead and make contact with Percy.

The sea was very choppy, and when cloud and mist came down it looked briefly as if we might be fog-bound. Then, quite suddenly, the mist lifted and the sun struggled to shine through the thinning clouds.

With his 10 horsepower engine going flat out Terry bravely pushed through the waves towards Fisherman's

Cove with the *Calamar* following behind, wallowing considerably. I was hoping to film our meeting with Percy but had to pack away my unhoused Bolex cine-camera to protect it from the water that poured into the tiny inflatable.

Much to my surprise we did not see Bob at our agreed rendezvous point. Failing to notice a group of people standing on the cliff top waving a yellow waterproof, we pressed on to Godrevy Island – but there was still no sign of Bob. Terry bravely took his tiny boat right round Godrevy Island. On the windward side the sea was huge, the big swell rising at times as high as a house alongside us while the white water boiled in the race between the island and the mainland. It was more than a little unnerving knowing that one's life depended upon a piece of inflated plastic and a tiny engine.

Out to sea, angry waves were pounding over the Stones. We could not risk taking the inflatable out that far, even though that was where the dolphin would be if he were not in-shore. But where was Bob?

Having circumnavigated Godrevy Island in the inflatable we headed back towards Portreath and the *Calamar* which was still battling its way forward. We ran alongside and I discussed the situation with the green-faced camera crew. Since it was far too dangerous to take the *Calamar* right out to the Stones, the fishing boat turned about and took a straight course back to Portreath while we followed the coastline close in-shore. In that way we would cover most of Percy's territory. We took aboard Mark's son Leif and continued the search, but arrived back at base without success. Putting our passenger ashore, we attempted to restart the engine but could not. We were extremely thankful it had not failed when we were out by Godrevy Island with a strong offshore wind. Terry changed the plug and eventually it fired again.

As the *Calamar* was still some way off I decided to scout in the opposite direction and thereby completely scan Percy's usual territory. We covered all the ground I had been to when I was out with Keith Pope on my very first reconnaissance to find Percy. Again, no luck, and no sign of Bob. Very disappointed we ran over to the *Calamar* which was chugging into Portreath Bay and escorted the fishing boat back into harbour.

I eventually did my interview standing beside a fishing boat on the sand in the dried-out harbour at Portreath. It made me aware once again just how privileged I had been in the past to spend so much time with Percy and Jean Louis. However, the 4.7 million viewers who eventually watched the programme were not completely deprived of seeing a wild dolphin, since Nick Heathcote, the director, inserted some sequences filmed by Laurie Emberson showing Percy curiously examining my light in Paradise Bay.

The next morning I called in at Beach House, to get a full account from Bob of his own search for Percy, and was greeted by Butch, the Holborns' black mongrel sheepdog, who was guarding the property in the absence of his masters. So I went in search of them and found Judy sitting in the Volvo looking out over Godrevy Island.

She told me that on the previous day Bob's engine had cut out quite suddenly, which left him with the problem of waiting for us or attempting to get to shore. He decided on the latter course, and with all three paddling as hard as they could they just made headway against the strong offshore wind and reached a tiny beach that had no footpath to it. Fortunately, someone had left a rope dangling down the cliff-face, and the three of them had managed to haul themselves up. They had seen us and frantically shouted and waved a yellow oilskin. But we had not noticed and their cries were carried away on the wind. Eventually they reached a telephone and Judy went and picked them up in the car.

As I spoke to Judy she told me that our old friend, Alan Vine, was out with Bob attempting to recover the Zodiac. When she had finished her story we looked out to sea, and there was the *Tar dor Moor*, with the inflatable in tow, heading back to Portreath.

I drove to Portreath Harbour and awaited Bob's arrival.

It was a sparkling day, the wind taking the tops off the white-crested waves like smoke.

Bob was very distressed when he learned that we had not found Percy. He said he had a feeling that the dolphin had moved away completely. It was therefore with considerable sadness that I left Portreath bathed in weak winter sunshine on 1 November, 1984.

I was awoken from sleep at home at 9.10 a.m. precisely three days later by telephone. It was a call from a diving friend, Warren Williams, who told me to switch on BBC Radio 4 immediately as there was a news item reporting the presence of a wild dolphin in St Ives Bay. Some of the Sunday papers also carried the news. Several people kindly contacted me and sent me cuttings.

It had taken exactly three days for the story to break and it took me two days to track down the man directly involved, on the evening of 5 November – Guy Fawkes' Day. I sat at the desk in my study and watched fireworks whizzing into the sky while I had a very long phone conversation with Joe Poynton in St Ives. During this time I was able to get first-hand the real story, which had been reported as 'SURFER JOE MEETS AN AMOROUS DOLPHIN' in the *Sunday Independent*, 'BEAKY'S BACK – AND HE'S STILL AMOROUS' in the *Western Evening Herald* and 'WHY THE AMOROUS DOLPHIN IS ALL AT SEA' in the *Daily Mail*.

Joe Poynton, an architect by profession, was an experienced sailor who had had many meetings with schools of dolphins on his voyages. He had met Donald, whom he called Beaky, when the dolphin was in the St Ives area in 1976 and 1977. Surprisingly, Joe had heard nothing about Percy and was therefore convinced that Donald had returned when a dolphin swam alongside his sailboard on Wednesday, 31 October, 1984. Joe was wearing a wetsuit and fell off his sailboard opposite the Coastguard Station. The dolphin enjoyed this turn of events, and with his penis exposed rubbed himself against the dunked windsurfer, who was dressed like a diver and was obviously at home in the sea.

This flurry of activity was watched by a coastguard. When he saw Joe trying to get back on to his board and being apparently pushed away by the dolphin, he telephoned Falmouth. The coastguard at Falmouth telephoned the lifeboat at St Ives, and the lifeboat went to Joe's rescue. The coastguard at Falmouth, who was also a reporter for the local radio station, telephoned the BBC in Truro, who announced the news. Joe was besieged by reporters. The following day he had more calls to his office about the dolphin than about business. By Saturday the national press had the story just in time for the Sunday papers.

The phone calls had almost petered out by the time I managed to speak to Joe. When I told him some of the antics Percy had got up to, he was in no doubt that the scarred dolphin who had been making amorous advances to him was not Beaky, alias Donald, but Portreath Percy. A case of mistaken identity.

So it transpired that on exactly the same day that Bob had had to abandon his boat, and I was being scared out of my wits in a tiny inflatable in huge waves around Godrevy Island, Percy was just three miles away in the relatively calm waters of St Ives Bay. And just to show who really was in charge, he created his own media event, having frustrated my attempts to film him with the BBC.

· 15 ·

A Gift From the Gods

During his stay off the Cornish coast from 1982 to 1984
Percy adopted a territory which included Godrevy Island
and the Stones. There was a definite cut-off line south-west
of Godrevy Island beyond which he appeared not to
venture. I had no reports of the presence of a friendly
dolphin off St Ives until he decided to disrupt Joe Poynton's
sailboarding activities. Crossing that line seemed to indicate that Percy was moving away. He has not been seen
since. At the time of writing, all the leads I have had have
been false. Where he went to from St Ives remains a
mystery. A person who claims to have been in touch with
Percy's spirit said that he has moved well away to join a
school of dolphins in the Azores. I hope she is correct.

Looking back objectively over all that has happened I can
find a natural explanation for such a move. I think Percy
was an adolescent who was nearly full grown but who had
not reached full sexual maturity when he first made contact
with humans in April 1982. I can as yet find no reason why
he should have adopted human company in preference to
that of his own kind at that stage in his life. But having done
so I think he found security in a familiar, well-defined area.
During the uncertain period of puberty he gained confidence in himself. As the result of his contact with humans
he discovered his superiority. And then, as humans have
done since earliest times, he set out to see the world.

I am fully aware that such an explanation is romantic and
anthropomorphic. But the truth of Percy's story is romantic, and to understand it I have to relate it to human actions

and values. I think we have to do likewise when attempting to understand the problems surrounding dolphin intelligence.

To do that I propose we must accept the premise that the brain is the focus of intelligence, and that having a brain equal in size to ours on a weight for weight basis endows a dolphin with a potential for aesthetic experience and intellectual thought processes as diverse and complex as those of a human. However, although there is some common ground, evolutionary and environmental differences between the two species have caused dolphins to utilise their higher mental processes in ways different from those of humans.

The divergence increased when humans first started to use tools, and has widened with the development of technology. The aboriginal Australians – who did not develop complex tools, whose nomadic life-style made possessions an impediment, and whose culture brought them into very close contact with the forces of nature – would have more in common with dolphins than would a white man brought up in an urban environment.

Thus dolphin intelligence is more closely related to aboriginal, independent, nomadic hunter-gatherer groups than is the intelligence that develops in humans brought up in urbanised, interdependent societies with static centres of very high population densities. The fact that some humans have successfully bridged the gap between the extremes of such cultures encourages me to believe that we can straddle the even greater divide between humans and dolphins.

The ground for such optimism is based on the belief that intelligence is at least partially dependent upon environment and upbringing. We know, for instance, that an Australian aborigine, brought up from birth exclusively in a Westernised society, is capable of academic achievements equal to those of his peers from other ethnic groups. If we reverse and extend this process, then it should be possible to gain a greater understanding of the workings of the mind of a dolphin by looking at the problem as an aborigine might

– i.e. in a non-mechanical, non-scientific way that relies more on intuitive feelings and senses than on predetermined analytical procedures. This is exactly what Tricia Kirkman did, quite unwittingly, when she swam with Percy and became aware that he was having a positive effect upon her emotions.

It is generally accepted that the spinal cord and the brain core are responsible for reflex reactions and that more advanced behaviour derives from complex interactions taking place between the core and the outer layers of the brain. Thus creatures with small brains, like sharks, are not capable of intricate behaviour such as play, which is engaged in by, among others, the aquatic mammals. However, while agreeing that larger brains endow the higher animals with greater capabilities, I would go one step further. I propose that the large, complex cerebral cortex which is uniquely common to dolphins and humans endows them with *special needs*.

These special needs are evident in Prehistoric man. Leakey and Lewin, in *People of the Lake*, observed that the first tool-makers not only made tools that were effective, but also went to considerable lengths to make them pleasing to hold and beautiful to look at. In other words, the tools were functional and also had aesthetic qualities. In modern man the needs that stem from the large cerebral cortex are satisfied by art, literature and music.

'Ah,' I hear you say. 'But the dolphins don't have literature, music and art.' I agree. So I suggest we should try to look through the eyes and minds of the aboriginal Australians. They had no written language, only the simplest of musical instruments and a few cave paintings. I think their higher aesthetic needs were satisfied by an unconscious appreciation of the natural beauty that surrounded them. I suggest, therefore, that the dolphins have a similar need which is satisfied by the experiences of roaming free in what to them is a beautiful environment.

If this is so, it begs an interesting question: 'Have humans created art forms to satisfy a basic need involving close contact with nature, which is denied them by the urban civilisation they have created with their hands?'

To help resolve that question I think we need to look at the way human intelligence develops, for it does not come instantly. It grows with the child. A two-year-old does not understand music, or how water turns to steam. Intelligence develops as the result of a continuous progression of problem-solving situations which commences the moment a baby is born. The experiences of the child have a profound and lasting effect on the way the adult tackles and resolves the problems of survival in later life. Also, the development of intelligence is inextricably linked with the process of education in its broadest sense. Familiarity plays a key role in both.

Most of us assume that we have an inherent appreciation of art forms and that this appreciation can be enjoyed by anyone with the necessary higher mental processes. But can it? Take music for example. Eastern music heard for the first time by a Westerner sounds discordant. When Tchaikovsky's Pathétique Symphony was first performed the composer was booed out of the auditorium. This failure to appreciate the music was due not to any lack of intelligence on the part of the audience but to their lack of familiarity with it. It took time and familiarity before the symphony was accepted as a masterpiece, and some say his greatest work.

So where does that place us when it comes to understanding and appreciating what goes on inside the brain of the dolphin, and to interpreting dolphin intelligence?

I think it means we must spend as much time as we possibly can flowing with dolphins in their natural environment and becoming familiar with their lives. We should observe them and relate to them with the minimum of interference. If we attempt to impose our will upon them and persuade them to perform for us, we will modify their behaviour to such an extent that we may end up destroying what we are looking for.

It was with these thoughts in mind that I reviewed what I

had set out to do and what I had achieved when Percy moved out of my orbit in November 1984. In terms of completing studies that could be written up like conventional scientific experiments (Introduction, Materials, Methods, Results and Conclusions), for which I had been trained and in which I had a great deal of experience, there was pathetically little. Indeed, if I was strictly honest and applied the major criteria by which such studies are judged by the scientific establishment, namely that they can be repeated and confirmed by other experimenters, then my results were tenuous and negative.

Even so, I felt I had made some progress which could not be defined in strictly scientific terms but none the less was positive and represented a real step forward. Was Carola right when she said that by setting out to do an experiment I was limiting what I could achieve?

To help unravel this possibility I asked myself some questions based on the assumption that dolphins were both sapient and sentient.

'If I had been working with an alien intelligence, would it react as predictably as a swinging pendulum, or a chemical reaction?' Answer, 'No.'

'Was I right to assume that the cooperative response I was looking for would be as precise and predictable as that of a platoon of soldiers under the command of a sergeant major?' Surely it was supreme arrogance on my part to assume that an intelligent, free-ranging, free-thinking animal would respond like a human. Answer, 'No.'

'Had the concepts so deeply ingrained by my years of training as a professional scientist become a fence around my mind blocking my view of the truth on the horizon?' Answer, 'I think this is highly likely.'

I felt I had to free my thoughts of pre-conceived notions if I was to succeed in isolating and identifying the quintessence of the dolphin nature from the mass of interactions I had experienced or witnessed with Jean Louis and Percy. So I let the memories of all that had happened tumble freely through my mind and tried to rationalise them – but not as a scientist. Then, one day, the answer jumped out at me.

I was looking after my nine-month-old grand-daughter, Rebecca. There was nobody else with us and we played together in a totally uninhibited manner. I quickly discovered what amused her and she immediately responded. She could tell if I was pleased or displeased and I knew when she was happy, when she was uncomfortable and when she was tired. In other words, we communicated but we did not pass the information to one another by comprehensible ordered speech. But the fact that we communicated was not important. It was *what* we communicated that was significant. She gave me her trust and at the same time her love. A love that was neither complicated with guilt nor distorted by prejudice. Her love was pure and innocent.

As I held her in my arms and we played together I realised that I had had the same kind of feelings before – when I was with Percy and Jean Louis. I then remembered how Tricia Kirkman described her feelings when she was being towed along by Percy, before the dolphin kissed her. Indeed, tears ran down her cheeks when she re-lived the moment. She said Percy did not love her for being fat or thin, old or young, male or female. He gave her an absolutely pure love that made her feel wonderful inside. There were no strings attached. It was a gift from the gods.

In recalling this incident I suffered the humiliating realisation that in one afternoon with only the minimum of contact with Percy a completely unqualified, non-scientific person, Tricia Kirkman, had instantly and intuitively achieved a greater understanding of dolphin psyche than I had in ten years of painstaking investigation. I had already recognised that she was an ultra-sensitive person. And it was this which enabled her to detect immediately the dolphin's special quality. I could not define it in scientific terms – but Tricia Kirkman called it simply *love*.

It was, and still is, as elusive as the beauty of a sunflower. With clinical drawings scientists can depict the petals and sepals, the phloem and xylem, and thereby define a sunflower. Yet it took a demented painter, Vincent van Gogh, who was completely unconcerned with facts, figures and experiments, to make me appreciate the beauty of a sunflower. Van Gogh also made me aware that as objects of beauty sunflowers may have more than additional sources of cooking oil to offer mankind.

In a paper in the Autumn 1985 issue of the journal *Metapsychology* there appeared a paper entitled 'The Percy Experience: Telepathic Communication with a Dolphin', by Sandra J. Stevens. It reported hypnosis sessions in which four subjects made contact with Percy's spirit and were asked to be made aware of the purpose of his mission off Cornwall. The outcome of the sessions was completely different for each subject, but a strong feeling of love was common to them all.

I think therein lies the key to the nature of the alien intelligence of the dolphin. The answer is that there is no single answer. Like the beauty of a sunflower, it is different to all men and women and therefore cannot be defined in precise scientific terms. However, that does not make it any the less real.

Postscript

The BBC received a huge response to *Eye of a Dolphin*, Lauric Emberson's film about Percy, when it was transmitted nationally on 12 March 1986. Many people wrote saying that it greatly uplifted their spirits. Their letters added to the accumulating evidence that dolphins have a beneficial effect on the emotional state of human beings, especially those suffering from depression.

I mentioned this while I was giving a film show at the Harbour House Hotel in Solva, in south-west Wales, where I was making a new film with Colin Stevens for HTV about a wild friendly dolphin named Simo. After the show I was asked if I would consider taking a man called Bill Bowell out to see the dolphin. I was told that Bill had been unable to work since 1974 when he had lost his job and had suffered a heart attack and a severe nervous breakdown. Despite the best medical treatment available in Oxford, where he lived, he had been unable to shake off his depression. His wife, Edna, and his family were in despair. There seemed little hope of Bill ever leading a normal life again. So I agreed to the request on the grounds that a boat trip at sea to meet Simo the dolphin could do no harm, and might even do some good.

Now, with the benefit of hindsight, I can see that that decision had consequences far beyond anything I could foresee at the time. It changed many lives – especially Bill's.

The next day was sullen and grey and seemed to match the unemotional look on Bill's face. Bill, locked in his own silent and haunted world, said little as he clambered aboard the large inflatable in yellow oilskins and we set off to see if we could find the dolphin. The boat wallowed and lurched over lead-coloured waves fringed with off-white foam that piled up round the entrance to the harbour, but our spirits rose when we were joined by the dolphin. Simo followed us as we motored towards the headland behind which we hoped to get out of the wind and into calmer water. There we anchored and Simo came alongside. Bill leaned over the side of the inflatable and stroked the dolphin's head.

'It was like I was in another world,' he said later. 'I wasn't aware of anyone around me at the time. Just touching the dolphin was magic.'

Bill then squeezed himself into one of my wetsuits and, holding on to the handline, rolled over the inflated wall of the rubber boat into the water. At first he was apprehensive, but his fear soon evaporated and he put his arm over the dolphin's head and hugged him. Whether the ungainliness of his entry into the water signalled to the dolphin that Bill was a novice I know not. What I do know is that there was an instant bond between the two of them the like of which I had not seen before.

'Simo nudged me from head to foot,' he later told Liz Johnson, a reporter from the *Oxford Courier*. 'The whole experience was one of beauty and quietness. It was as though I was being told – "you've been in your silent world for a few years, but I've been in mine all my life."'

Even when the dolphin dislodged his mask and snorkel Bill was not distressed. He felt the dolphin was telling him, 'You're safe with me. You don't need this.'

Bill's wife Edna added her own comment. 'Bill was completely relaxed when he came out of the water: he was so happy, and his whole expression had changed.'

The film I made about Simo, called *Bewitched by a Dolphin*, recorded the magical effect the dolphin had upon the inhabitants of Solva and its visitors, including Tricia Kirkman. Her life had been transformed by meeting the wild dolphin Percy, and on the day after Bill's encounter we stood together on the cliffs overlooking the harbour, watching him help people on to the boat and chatting amiably as they left the harbour. Previously he had been reluctant to leave the hotel. The skipper even let Bill steer the boat. Best of all Bill was *smiling*. A happy, carefree smile.

'Bill has blossomed like a sunflower,' Tricia said. 'Wouldn't it be lovely if we could have boatloads of sunflowers like him, all meeting dolphins?'

That was the moment in which 'Operation Sunflower' was born. I decided to see if I could discover why dolphins have such a powerful influence on people suffering from depression. I had long been convinced that nature can provide relief from, and sometimes the cure for many ailments if only we can find the key. Aspirin, the most widely used drug in the world, is present in the bark of willow trees. Tuberculosis killed tens of thousands of people in the nineteenth century, yet a remedy (penicillin) was found in a green mould that grows on cheese and stale bread. So, I asked myself, do the dolphins possess some special quality which can change the human psyche for the better? Indeed, was this why dolphins were deified in the past? Did the Ancient Greeks know something which has since been smothered by the progress of our so-called civilisation in which most life-styles have been progressively removed from intimate contact with the forces of nature?

It appeared to me that dolphins radiate a force, a field of influence, an aura, something, call it what you will, that could change our states of consciousness. But could I investigate and evaluate it?

One thing I knew I had to take into account was the fact that I myself would not be able to experience the profound mood changes that might take place in people suffering from depression, simply because I was not a chronic depressive – in the same way that I might experience no noticeable effect from taking an antibiotic if I was not suffering from a bacteriological disease. Only the victims of depression would be able to confirm or deny my hypothesis.

I was utterly opposed to using dolphins in captivity. So in practical terms I was confined to working with wild dolphins which deliberately sought the company of humans. On that score at least I had the cooperation of Simo – or I did until quite suddenly he disappeared without trace shortly after I had decided to embark on 'Operation Sunflower'.

Now one of the advantages of being known as 'The Dolphin Man' is that people contact me and tell me of their own dolphin stories. John O'Connor wrote to me from the little Irish fishing village of Dingle in County Kerry, where a dolphin was escorting the fishing boats in and out of the harbour. Divers had been able to get into the water with her, he told me. Then, as so often happens in my life, the right person turned up at just the right time. After doing a long interview for BBC Radio Humberside my interviewer, Jon Levy, proposed a way of making available the necessary resources for the launch of 'Operation Sunflower'. As a result, I was able to take Bill and a film crew to Ireland to meet the dolphin in the summer of 1987. With Bill were two much younger people whose depression showed itself in different forms: Jemima suffered from *anorexia nervosa* and could not stop starving herself; Neal was sometimes so incapacitated by the fear of facing the day that he could not climb out of the bath in the morning or do up his shoelaces. Both were intelligent youngsters who could not respond when urged simply to pull themselves together. They had nothing so visible as a broken leg, but their medical problems were real enough.

We recorded the effect the dolphin had on these three people and their effect on the dolphin. At the end of the year I showed a short clip of this film in the Dome at Brighton during the International Underwater Film Festival, where it had a most moving effect on the audience. It ended with Bill swimming to the side of the inflatable and saying, 'I wish I could become a merman.' For Bill, the encounter was more therapeutic than all the anti-depressant tablets he had taken over more than a decade.

He talked with great feeling of his Dingle dolphin experience to Liz Johnson, who concluded her article in the *Oxford Courier* with his words: 'It's a pity you can't bottle dolphins and put them into every psychiatric ward in the country.'

Now that last statement is not as absurd as it sounds. We all know that it is possible to capture with quite simple technology the mood-changing magic of music and to re-create it when and where we wish. Just what can be done to synthesise the magic of dolphins is something which will come more fully to light as 'Operation Sunflower' progresses.

And that will be the subject of my next book.